Tag
The Rebellion Series

Nicola Jane

Copyright © 2019 by Nicola Jane

Copyright © 2023 by Nicola Jane

All rights reserved.

No portion of this book may be reproduced in any form without written permission from the publisher or author, except as permitted by U.K. copyright law.

Meet the Team

Cover Designer: Francessca Wingfield, Wingfield Designs
Editor: Rebecca Vazquez, Dark Syde Books
Proofreader: Jackie Ziegler, Dark Syde Books
Formatting: Nicola Miller

Spelling Note:

Please note, this author resides in the United Kingdom and is using British English. Therefore, some words may be viewed as incorrect or spelled incorrectly, however they are not.

Disclaimer:

This book is a work of fiction. The names, characters, places, and incidents are all products of the author's imagination and are not to be construed as real. Any similarities are entirely coincidental.

Tag was previously released as Rebellion MC book One in 2019.

Acknowledgments

For my readers who continue to read what I write, support me, and send me lovely messages. Thank you. x

Trigger Warning

♥

This book comes with a trigger warning, although if you read mafia or MC romance, you'll already know what to expect.

Tag contains some scenes that readers may consider as cheating (I do not) There is mild violence, lot's of terrible words (unsuitable for the faint hearted) and an MMA fighter with a bad attitude.

Enter at your own risk...

Contents

Social Media	IX
Playlist	X
Chapter One	1
Chapter Two	10
Chapter Three	17
Chapter Four	28
Chapter Five	37
Chapter Six	46
Chapter Seven	54
Chapter Eight	67
Chapter Nine	77
Chapter Ten	90
Chapter Eleven	100
Chapter Twelve	112
Chapter Thirteen	121
Chapter Fourteen	131

Chapter Fifteen	139
Chapter Sixteen	151
Chapter Seventeen	162
Chapter Eighteen	170
Chapter Nineteen	178
Chapter Twenty	186
Chapter Twenty-One	192
Chapter Twenty-Two	200
Epilogue	205
A note from me to you	208
Popular Books by Nicola Jane	210

Social Media

♥

I love to hear from my readers and if you'd like to get in touch, you can find me here . . .

My Website: https://authornicolajane.com/

My Facebook Page

My Facebook Readers Group

Bookbub

Instagram

Goodreads

Amazon

Playlist

Trouble – Coldplay
Womanizer – Britney Spears
Leave (Get Out) – JoJo
Sex on Fire – Kings Of Leon
Troublemaker – Olly Murs
Too Little, Too Late – JoJo
Fall In Love Alone – Stacey Ryan
Only Love Can Hurt Like This – Paloma Faith
SNAP – Rosa Linn
Don't Blame Me – Taylor Swift
Unstoppable – Sia
FIGURES – Jessie Reyez
Wicked Game – Grace Carter
DO YOU LOVE HER – Jessie Reyez
Break Your Heart (Remix) – Taio Cruz ft. Ludacris
Hot N Cold – Katy Perry
I Knew You Were Trouble. – Taylor Swift
i hate u, i love u – Gnash ft. Olivia O'Brien
New Rules – Dua Lipa

Chapter One

LUCY

"I heard that after the fight, Tag sends out his security to pick women for him." My best friend, Tyra, flicks her black hair over her shoulder. Her large brown eyes dart around before she adds, "Yah know, for sex or something."

"That's disgusting. If a man can't be bothered to approach me himself, then he isn't worth my time," says Maribel firmly.

"That's why you're single, Bel." I grin, popping a straw into my glass of gin and giving it a stir. "Why doesn't he just come and talk with a girl he likes?"

"He's tipped to be the next big thing," says Tyra. "I guess being that popular with the ladies kind of makes you big-headed."

We take our drinks from the bar and push through the crowd to find our table. It's Friday night and my girls dragged me on a night out. Tyra is a journalist, and she gets the best gossip on celebrities, but she also drags us to a lot of functions so she can grab the next story. Tonight, for example, an up-and-coming MMA fighter by the name of Tag is in the ring. Tyra managed to get us front row seats, which she was really excited about, but personally, I'm not into watching men beat the crap out of each other.

I choose a chair farthest from the cage. I'd heard horror stories from my assistant at work about getting splattered by blood. He was probably just kidding, but I don't want to take the risk.

"How's Noah?" asks Bel. She always asks to be polite, but my two friends hate my boyfriend. They think he's an arrogant arse.

"Busy with work," I say with a shrug. It's my classic response when they ask me because I know they aren't really interested, they're just being good friends.

"Oh my god, he's over there," says Tyra excitedly while tapping Bel on the arm. I crane my neck to try and spot whoever she's pointing at. It's not like Tyra to get excited, she meets celebrities all the time. "He's so gorgeous," she gushes, practically swooning.

The crowd parts slightly, and I spot a large guy covered in tattoos. I don't think there's one part of exposed skin that's not covered in art. His hair is cropped short, shaved at the sides and slightly longer on top. His dark facial stubble adds to his sexiness. I like my men clean cut and shaven, but there's something about this man that gets my blood pumping.

"He definitely has something about him," Bel says, sighing dreamily.

"Can we take a moment to appreciate those muscles? The guy is ripped!" says Tyra.

I watch as he makes his way towards us, occasionally stopping by a table and chatting with the occupants. A female rushes past our table, headed straight for Tag. She hands him a pen and pulls down her top, so he can sign his autograph across her chest.

"I wonder if he's girl spotting now," Tyra muses, running her fingers through her hair and crossing her long legs. Tag passes our table without giving any of us a second glance. Tyra looks positively outraged. "Rude!"

I exchange a smirk with Bel. Only Tyra would be insulted that she wasn't picked out like a piece of meat.

The night drags. I've already drunk far too much, and Tag's fight is only just beginning. My mobile vibrates on the table, and I glance down at a text from Noah telling me he's gone for a few drinks with his business partners. *Whatever, he's never home anyway.*

I try to get enthusiastic about the two men battering each other in the cage, but I just don't see the pleasure in it. Tyra was right—Tag is good. He hardly has a mark on him while the other guy is a bloody mess.

When it's finally over a few minutes later, the crowd erupts with excitement as Tag holds his hands up in glory. While all the fuss around me is playing out, a man in a suit approaches me. He leans into my ear and says, "Tag invites you to an exclusive club after the fight." He pushes a small white card into my hand. "Your friends are welcome to join you." And then he walks away. I frown, watching him disappear into the crowd, then I look down at the card. It's expensive-looking, with black lettering in the centre, showing an address and the number ten.

Ten minutes later, we step from the fight club onto the wet, cold streets of London. The rain drizzles, and I know if we don't hurry to get a cab, my curly dark hair will soon be frizzy and flat. Tyra waves her hand frantically until a black cab pulls over, and we all pile in. "Where to, ladies?" asks the driver, his London accent thick.

"Actually, I have this." I show the card to Tyra. "You can drop me home and then head on there if you're looking to party your night away." I don't fancy schmoozing at Tag's afterparty, but Tyra could get an exclusive story out of it.

"Oh my god, is this what I think it is?" she asks, staring down at the little white card.

"A man in a suit gave it to me at the end of the fight."

"Well, we have to go. You, too."

"Erm, no, it really doesn't sound like something I want to go to," I say firmly.

"Oh, come on, Lucy, you used to love a good party," she argues.

"Leave her, Ty. She doesn't like that stuff anymore. It's not her *scene*," says Bel. I don't miss the way she raises her eyebrows when she says the word 'scene'.

"That's not fair," I argue. "I just don't feel like it tonight."

"Because it's not full of your kind of people," says Tyra.

"Look, I hate to butt in here, girls, but if you're not gonna give me an address, would you mind stepping out of the cab so I can get on with my work," says the driver.

"Yah know what, fine, let's go to the stupid party." I flop back into the seat, folding my arms across my chest and glaring out the window.

It's no secret that I come from a wealthy family. My stepfather is CEO of a large energy company. Since the world went crazy for global change, he's been raking in the cash, selling energy saving solutions to large businesses. My boyfriend, Noah, has a similar background to me. We met in college four years ago, when he was studying law. He's now a partner in his father's law firm and was recently featured in *Time Business News* as one of the new up-and-coming lawyers this year.

I don't make a show of my wealth. In fact, I avoid it at all costs. I went to college, and now, I have my own business as a wedding and party planner. My stepfather wasn't impressed with my career choice, and Noah often refers to it as my little project to keep me busy. I don't care, I love it and it's mine. I worked hard for it, and I even went to the bank to get the starter loan, refusing to take my family's money.

"Sorry, Luce, we were just kidding," mutters Tyra. I met the girls in school when we were five years old, long before my mother met my stepfather. I was twelve when they moved me to a private school, but I kept in touch with the girls.

"I hate how you always do that when you don't get your own way. You use that against me. You know the real me, you know I hate all that, and it's so shit that as my friends, you bring it up to make me do what you want."

Tyra takes my hand. "You're right, I'm so sorry. We'll take you home first."

"No, we're almost there now. Noah isn't home anyway," I mutter sulkily.

"He's not home?" asks Bel.

"Drinks with the partners at work," I say. The girls raise their eyebrows but choose wisely not to comment.

The cab stops outside a swanky-looking hotel. Tyra wipes the condensation from the window and peers outside. "Are you sure this is the right place?" she asks.

"I've been a cab driver for twenty years, love. I never fuck it up. This is the place." We step out, handing the driver the fare.

"I've never been inside this place before," Tyra mutters, running for the shelter of the doorway.

"It's expensive here," I say. I'd heard about it from Penelope, one of my 'rich' friends. Her husband owned a huge accounting firm in central London, and they would often have dinner here to impress clients.

I enter first, my heels clicking on the shiny, white marble floor. The receptionist glances up and smiles widely. "Welcome to Hotel Martinez. How may I help you this evening?" Her perfectly straight, white teeth almost gleam against her well made-up face.

"I have this," I tell her, handing over the card.

The receptionist glances at the card and gives a nod. "Take the golden elevator to the top floor. Enjoy your evening."

Inside the elevator, there's a plush purple seat and a large golden mirror. Tyra snaps a picture on her mobile. "Seriously, it's just a seat," I say with a laugh.

"I've never been in an elevator like it. Someone could actually live in this thing, it's so big."

"What do you think the number ten means on the card?" asks Bel.

I shrug. "Maybe a room number? It has to be something obvious because the receptionist knew exactly what it was."

The elevator stops smoothly and the doors slide open to reveal a large foyer. We step out and glance around at the expensive area. Large paintings are displayed on the white walls. The carpet is a deep purple colour, and there are four chaise lounges with golden legs spread around. "Well, this looks promising," notes Bel.

"I was expecting a nightclub, or a bar at least. We're not going to know anyone in here," I say cautiously. "It's all a little weird."

"It's exclusive, Lucy, relax. It's exciting," Tyra says, stepping towards a large double door. She knocks, and my heart almost beats out of my chest. I hate doing stuff like this. No one knows where we are or who we're with—we could be murdered in there. The door opens and a man in a suit pops his head out. "Hey, we have a card," says Tyra, holding her hand out to me, so I can pass her the card. She holds it up for him to inspect, and he gives a nod, holding the door wider for us to step inside. The room is just as amazing as the foyer, and Bel gasps aloud, earning her a scowl from Tyra, who I think is pretending she attends these sorts of things all the time.

There are lots of people inside—men in suits with glasses in their hands, and women huddled in groups, drinking Champagne. There's a low beat indicating there's music in here somewhere, but it's not loud enough for me to make out the song. "Well, this is hardly an afterparty," I mutter.

Tyra scowls at me. "I just want some pictures and then we can go," she hisses. "If I get a good story, my boss might actually like me for a day." Tyra got a job for *The London Gazette* when she left college at eighteen. Her boss is a prick, always making Tyra feel like she's incompetent.

A waitress passes holding a tray of Champagne, and before I can take one, a man steps back, knocking into the her. The tray tilts and the glasses slide off, hitting the floor one after the other. "Holy shit," I gasp, jumping out of the way to avoid the splashes of sticky liquid.

The waitress apologises profusely, crouching down to pick up shards of broken glass. "It's fine, it wasn't your fault," I reassure her, also bending to give her a helping hand.

The guy who knocked into her huffs loudly, wiping down his jacket with a white handkerchief. "Incompetent little wench," he grumbles.

"It was your fault," I snap. The waitress touches my hand gently and shakes her head in warning.

"Please, it's fine," she says quietly.

The crowd parts slightly, and a large man stomps through. He reaches down and grips the girl by the top of her arm, wrenching her from her crouching position so that she stands before him. She immediately hangs her head low and apologises. I rise to my feet, wiping my hands on my thighs. "It wasn't her fault," I say firmly, and the man's sharp, dark eyes turn to me. He's scowling, his face red and mean-looking. "That guy bumped into her."

"And you are?" he growls.

"A guest," I snap, placing my hand on my hips, "And a founding member of 'Treat your staff well', yah dick," I add. I hear Bel snigger behind me.

"And you were invited here by?" he presses, choosing to ignore my comment. I hold the card up, and the guy smirks slightly. "Oh, number ten." I frown in confusion, but then the crowd parts again and my breath catches in my throat. Tag is standing before me, freshly showered, his hair damp. A black T-shirt clings to his tight muscles, and it's tucked neatly into his Levi's. I silently beg for him to turn around so I can check out his backside in those bad boys.

"What's going on?" he asks, giving the man a hard stare. I'm slightly offended that he hasn't addressed me, seeing as it was obvious that I was talking to the guy first.

"Sorry, Tag. This idiot spilled a tray of Champagne, showering your guests."

"I'm so sorry, Mr. Corallo," whispers the girl, tears in her eyes. "It was an accident. I'll pay for the damage."

"Shit," I huff, "I'll pay for the damage if it means so damn much." I reach into my purse and pull out a handful of money. I'm not sure how much is there, but I'm sure it will be enough. I stuff it in the man's jacket pocket and pat it for good measure. "If it's any more than that, I'll write a check. Now, let the girl go," I say.

Tag smirks and raises his eyebrow. "You heard the lady, let her go," he says. The large guy releases the waitress, annoyance crossing his features. "Now, get the mess cleared away," he adds. The waitress goes about picking up the glass, and I'm about to help her when Tag steps closer. "You are?" he asks.

"Lucy," I mutter, my face flushing crimson.

"Where's your card, Lucy?" he asks. I hold it up, and he smirks again. "Hmm, number ten. Okay, let's go." He turns his back to me and starts to push through the crowd. I glance to Tyra and Bel, who are staring after him wide-eyed.

"Well, go then," says Tyra, shoving me forward. I dig my heels in.

"No way!" I almost screech. "I don't even know the guy. Where's he wanna take me? And what's the significance of the number?"

"Who cares? He's a god among men, so follow him," encourages Bel. Instead, I bend my knees and help the waitress pick up the broken glass. I don't know who the hell Tag is, or what that number means, and I don't think I want to find out.

Chapter Two

TAG

I make my way through the room, occasionally stopping to shake hands and accept congratulations for tonight's win. I get to the bedroom and turn around to find number ten is nowhere in sight. *What the actual fuck?* Antonio is standing by the wall, watching the room. He's head of my security, not that I need all that shit. "Where did number ten go?" I ask.

He shrugs and then speaks into his mouthpiece, asking for the other guys to find number ten and bring her over. I spot number fifteen and smile. "Forget it, Tony. I'll take her instead." I saunter over, and she smiles when she spots me. I feel like a lion playing with its prey. "Number fifteen, step this way." She giggles, and the sound irritates me, but I guess I'll suck it up just to get ahead of Anton.

Fifteen steps into my room and looks around, her eyes wide with hunger. Another money-grabber, but if that's what gets them in here, then I don't give a shit. "This place is lovely," she says, running a well-manicured hand along the four-poster bed in the centre of the room.

I nod towards the lone standing bathtub over the far side of the room. The water is hot, and pink rose petals float on top. "Let's have a soak, my muscles are tight." I wink, and she grins wider as she pulls at the tie around her waist. The knot unfastens easily, and the dress falls open, revealing white lace underwear. I inhale sharply at the sight of her perfect body, glad that this one isn't covered in fake tan. I pull my T-shirt over my head and throw it on a chair, and then I kick off my shoes and push the jeans down my legs. Fifteen strips out of her underwear, and I watch the sway of her perfectly rounded arse as she sashays over to the bathtub. Call me weird, but I have a thing about girls being clean before I go there. She steps into the water and lowers herself gracefully until just her head pokes out of the water.

I step out of my boxers, and her eyes follow me as I approach. I know I look good—my body is tight and my muscles in top shape with tattoos crawling across my skin. I'm not exactly small in *that* area either. In fact, it's been a bit of a curse.

I climb into the tub behind Fifteen and pull her back against my front. The feel of her wet, silky skin against my own gets me hard instantly, and she gasps as my erection presses into her back. I run my hands across her flat stomach and up towards her breasts. They're easily a D cup, and as I massage them in my palms, I'm disappointed to feel that they aren't real. I have nothing against fake breasts, but occasionally it'd be nice to feel a real pair, something that seems to be rare these days.

Fifteen places her hands on my knees and uses the leverage to rub herself up and down against me. I close my eyes and rest my head back against the tub. She feels nice, way better than number twelve. As Fifteen turns and rests on her knees, water and bubbles run down her breasts, and I have the urge to lick them. She grips my erection and begins to run her wet hands up and down the length. I glance at the bowl of condoms over by the bed. I can't let Fifteen near me without one, and I know she wants to taste me because she's licking her lips hungrily. I still her hands, and she looks up at me. "Let's take this over to the bed," I say. She nods in agreement, and I sigh in relief.

We don't bother with towels. Fifteen falls onto the bed and begins to rub herself. I watch as I rip open the condom wrapper. Fuck, she's hot. I grab my mobile phone and snap a photo of her while her eyes are closed in ecstasy, and then I crawl between her legs and line myself up with her entrance. Fifteen wraps one leg around my waist and pulls me forward so that I'm easing into her. She groans in pleasure and wraps her hands around my head, trying to pull me in for a kiss. Another no, no, so I distract her by kissing up her neck instead. This pacifies her enough until I'm in as far as I can go without making her uncomfortable.

I begin to pull back out, taking her hands in my own and pinning them above her head. I need to take control, or she'll have her mouth attached to mine in no time. Once I'm satisfied that she's secured beneath me, I begin to pump in and out, my pace hard and fast. Sweat beads on my brow and chest. My muscles were already on fire after my fight, and this is my second fuck of the night.

I squeeze my eyes shut and picture Ella, her brown hair, her gorgeous plump lips, her... my image of Ella disappears, and instead, I'm staring at the image of number ten. It's her dark bouncy hair and pink lips that fill my mind, and before I know it, I'm growling through an intense orgasm. My movements are jerky, and the warm feeling that courses through me is something I've not experienced before.

"Fuck, fuck, fuck," repeats Fifteen, biting her lip between her teeth. She shudders and bucks off the bed, her own orgasm controlling her body. I slow my movements, panting hard as my heart beats out of my chest. I roll off of Fifteen and flop onto my back. Where the hell did that image come from? I must have looked at the girl for all of twenty seconds, and yet, I had the perfect picture of her in my head. I only come when I picture Ella . . . it's always been Ella.

I wipe the sweat from my brow with the back of my hand. The bed shifts beside me and Fifteen curls into my side, her breasts pressing against my ribs. "Wow," she mutters, sleepily. I sit up, putting some distance between us, and reach for my Levi's. "What are you doing?" she asks.

"There's a party out there. You need to get your shit together and get gone." I make sure my voice is cold and clear. Fifteen sits up, not at all bothered by her naked body.

"Seriously?"

"And don't think of spreading rumours. I have a photograph of you fingering yourself, and it isn't pretty."

She dives from the bed, rage on her face. "Are you being serious?" she yells, grabbing her underwear and pulling them on. "You're just gonna kick me out of here?"

"Yeah, I don't revisit. Thanks for a great time, though, and remember what I said, no rumours." I pull on my T-Shirt, and when my head pops through the hole, Fifteen is waiting. Her hand stings my cheek as she hits me hard. I hiss and then smile. It's all part of it—I've lost count of the number of slaps I've received. In fact, it became so regular that we started adding an extra point. So, Fifteen has become Sixteen. Bonus!

I leave the room so Sixteen can get dressed and make her exit with a little more dignity. Finding Anton at the bar, he smirks at me. "Sixteen," I say, fist-bumping him. "She got the extra point."

"Thought she looked like a whore." Anton smiles, offering me a whiskey, which I take gratefully.

"What's the deal with number ten?" I ask casually. "Why Ten?"

Anton thinks for a moment and then laughs. "Oh right, she was a last minute. My original Ten couldn't make the party, so I had the card spare. I happened past the table and spotted her. She's maybe a twelve at a push, but beggars can't be choosers. Her friends weren't too bad either. I regret not spotting them earlier."

"Man, you're too harsh with your scoring. She was easily an eighteen, maybe higher," I mutter, knocking my drink back.

"Oh, do I detect a note of attraction?" mocks Anton.

"God, no, I'm just saying I thought ten was a little low."

"Isn't that her?" asks Anton, nodding to the other side of the small bar. I watch as Ten orders herself a drink, a rum and Coke. "Can you manage a third? It's getting to the end of the month, and let's not forget who's winning this time," says Anton, grinning mischievously.

"Well, sometimes you need to win. It's not fair if I take the glory every time." I'm lying, of course. I'm hugely competitive, especially when it comes to me and Anton. We've been friends since we were kids, when I stuck up for him in a fight. Not that he needed it—his family name was enough to scare anyone away.

I had to win this time. My new Rolex was at stake. It had been a present to myself after my tenth win in a row.

"I'll tell you what. I'll give you thirty points if you win her tonight."

I glance at Anton, dubious of his intentions. He never gives away extra points. "What do you get out of it?" I ask.

"Nothing, I know what that watch means to you. I have a heart, yah know."

I scowl. Anton doesn't have a heart, but we're like brothers, and so I believe what he's saying. Thirty points would put us on an even score. I've been lacking this month because I'd been training so hard for this fight. I hold my hand out, and we shake on it. "Thirty-five if you get her to agree to both of us," he adds with a wink. "You're right, she's worth more than ten."

I walk away, shaking my head and laughing. Moving to stand close behind number Ten, I'm practically stuck to her back, and when she leans over the bar to speak to the bartender, her arse presses against my cock and I close my eyes. After starving myself of sex for two weeks in preparation for the fight, I could definitely go all night.

Ten glances back over her shoulder, and it's sexy and alluring. When she sees it's me, she scowls. "Tag."

"Ten. You didn't follow me."

"Was I supposed to? And my name is Lucy, not ten."

"Yes, Ten, you were supposed to. You missed out. I had a red-hot bubble bath, rose petals, and a four-poster bed with your name on it."

"My actual name or number ten?" she queries, tipping her head to the side. I smirk. She's got a smart mouth, I like it. "And FYI, I hate roses."

"I'll call my guy, get them removed. What do you like? I'll fill the room."

"My god, you're smooth," she mutters and then turns back to the bartender.

"You're making the most of the free bar," I say, noting it's her second rum and Coke in less than five minutes.

"Don't have a free bar if you don't want people to use it," she says coldly, then she moves around me, and I follow her. She stops near her friends, who are huddled on a couch, all staring at a mobile phone. "Why are you following me?" she asks.

"I'm not following you. It's my party, I'm mingling."

"If you get any closer, you'll be up my arse." I wiggle my brows, and she gives me a disgusted look.

"You didn't tell me your favourite flower."

"You could fill that room with gold bars and I wouldn't go into it with you. Goodbye, Tag."

"I doubt that very much," I mutter, but she doesn't hear.

Instead, she turns back to her friends. "I'm gonna go home. This party is boring," she says, "and Noah will probably be home by now."

"Who's Noah?" I ask. Her friends watch the exchange as Ten turns back to me.

"Will you please go away?" she hisses. "You are so irritating."

"You're an ice queen," I retort. "I was being friendly."

"No, you were trying to get me into your room by flashing your cash. Not all girls melt at a cheap bunch of rose petals, and not all girls drop their knickers at good looks and tattoos. I have a boyfriend, so back off."

I hold my hands up and take a step back. Not many girls knock me back, and I'm surprised how much it turns me on. Ten doesn't realise but she's made herself a target because I have thirty-five points riding on her arse, and I'm sure with a little convincing, I can get Anton to raise the stakes.

Chapter Three

LUCY

I unlock my apartment door and step inside. "Hello," I call out. Noah doesn't answer, just like he didn't answer my texts asking if he was home yet. I drop my purse and my shoes by the door and go straight for the kitchen. I need water before tonight's alcohol makes a reappearance.

The silence is shattered two minutes later when the door flies open and Noah stumbles inside. He almost trips over my purse and shoes, despite the fact they were to the side. "Fuck, Lucy, move your shit," he yells, picking up my shoes and throwing them across the room. I place my glass in the sink and take a deep breath. Sometimes he gets like this if he's had too much to drink.

"Did you have a good night?" I ask, turning to face him as he stumbles towards the kitchen.

"No. Jackson Preston was on my arse all night about a case I know fuck all about because my assistant is fucking useless," he growls. "I looked like an idiot. I'm gonna fire that bitch on Monday."

I reach for his tie and loosen it slightly, pressing a hand to his chest to steady him. "I'm sure you didn't. You're the best lawyer I know."

"And how many do you know, Lucy?" he snaps. "Did you call my mother to speak with her about the dress situation for tomorrow night?" I inwardly cringe because I forgot. "Don't tell me you forgot again."

"I was crazy busy at work today. It slipped my mind." Noah closes his eyes and takes a deep, calming breath. I step back, knowing he might lose his shit any second.

"Busy at playing party planning?" he sneers. "Yet you found time to see your friends."

"I'll call her first thing. If we clash, then I'll find something else," I say brightly. "It's not the end of the world."

It was the wrong thing to say, and Noah's hand strikes me hard across the face. "It is the end of the fucking world if you make me look like an idiot, Lucy. It's important and you know it is. This awards evening has been planned for weeks, and as usual, you leave everything to the last minute."

I grip my cheek. It burns, and I bite back a response about visible bruising. "Sorry, Noah."

"Sorry," he repeats, adding a menacing laugh. "Come on, Lucy, that's not like you." He's baiting me, like he always does when he's drunk. He grabs hold of my top, using it to pull me towards him. "You disgust me," he hisses into my face.

"You're overreacting, Noah. Let's go to bed and talk about this in the morning." His hand moves to my hair and he grips a handful at the base of my skull. "Please, Noah."

"Please, Noah. I'm sorry, Noah," he says, mocking me. "Always so fucking sorry. Well, you'd better show me how sorry you are," he growls, ripping my top open. I shove him away, trying to make a run for it, but he's too quick and he gets a grip of my hair again. This time, he pulls it hard so my head tilts back. I slap his face, hoping this brings him around, but instead, it angers him more. He bites my arm, drawing blood, and I cry out, slapping him again, this time using my nails to scratch him.

"Stop," I yell. I pull free again and run so fast, my feet can't keep up. I slip on the tiles and crash to the floor, hitting the side of my head hard. I feel dizzy for a few seconds, and Noah takes full advantage. He's on top of me, his weight crushing me. Holding my face against the floor, he then flips me over so I'm on my stomach. I try desperately to scramble to my knees, but he presses his hand into the centre of my back. He tugs at my jeans, but the button holds tight, making it hard for him to get them down without releasing my arm. I know that as soon as he does, I'm going to push to my knees and escape. A loud bang on the door startles us both. I still, panting. Noah crouches down so he's closer to my ear and growls, "Don't fucking move." I wait for him to get off me and go to answer the door before I pull myself up from the floor.

When Noah opens it, his father pushes his way in. He glances between us suspiciously, and I know he sees it—the resemblance in the pair of them is too similar for him not to see what this is. He presses his lips together in a tight line and then turns to face Noah. "I was on my way home and realised that I didn't leave the keys with you. You'll get in earlier than me tomorrow." He holds out a large bunch of keys, and Noah takes them.

"Thanks."

"How are you, Lucy?" he asks.

"I'm good. I was just leaving, actually," I say, picking up the shoes that Noah had thrown across the room.

"No, Lucy, wait," says Noah, stepping forward. His father places a hand on his chest, halting him from approaching me. "Lucy, please."

"I'll call you tomorrow, Noah," I say, adding a fake smile and grabbing my purse. Noah works every weekend, so he won't be home all day tomorrow. I'll return once he's gone.

I walk for ten minutes. Luckily, our apartment is just a short walk from central London, and I make my way to my usual hotel. Friendly and discreet, I always end up here when Noah gets a little crazy. The night receptionist smiles when she sees me and taps away on her computer. "Room ten is available," she says.

I hand over my credit card, and she swipes it in her machine. Room ten ... how ironic that the number ten keeps popping up today. Once she has my card details, she hands me the key card. "I'll arrange for some nightwear to be brought up." I nod gratefully and head towards the elevator.

I have a great sleep, one where I dream of the mysterious Tag from last night. I wake to an annoying buzzing sound and reach for my bag, fishing around inside until I find my phone. Opening one eye, I see Penelope's name and groan. If I ignore the call, she'll get pissed, and I'm counting on her company tonight at this ridiculous awards ceremony.

"Penelope, good morning," I say as brightly as I can manage.

"Do you need a makeup artist for this evening?" she asks, straight to the point like always.

"No, I can do my makeup," I say, confused.

"I'm assuming you're not in your apartment because Noah turned Hulk on you last night," she says, and I roll my eyes.

"How do you know I'm not in my apartment?"

"Because I'm standing outside of it knocking on your door."

"Maybe I met a hunky man to rescue me. What time is it anyway?"

"It's ten. Did you sort out your dress? I heard Noah's mother is wearing dusky pink," she says. "How very nineties," she adds, and I smile. Penelope may be a stuck-up cow, but she has my back when it comes to Noah and his family. She's the only one who knows how Noah can be when he's drunk. She knows the signs because Wyatt, her husband, is the same, so when she questioned me one time, I didn't have the strength to lie.

"I need a dress," I groan.

"I'll come and get you. The usual spot?"

"Yes." I sigh. "Thanks, Pen."

Twenty minutes later, I step from the hotel and Penelope is waiting across the street. Her designer shades are firmly in place even though it's a cold day. Her silk scarf is wrapped loosely around her neck, and her long, oversized coat hangs from her shoulders. She looks every bit of class. "Wow, nice," she says, taking my chin in her cold hand and turning my face to the side. "You will need a makeup artist."

"I need a new boyfriend," I mutter.

"Hmm, I don't see that being an easy breakup." She's right, mine and Noah's family are very close, despite Noah's mother hating me for reasons I have yet to discover. Our parents often speak of a wedding for us, but I think that has more to do with two rich families linking together rather than anything love-related.

"Right, let's head to Bond Street," says Penelope, linking arms with me and dragging me in that direction.

I hate dress shopping. I've had to put up with it since my mother married my stepfather over ten years ago. He's always gone to fancy parties and charity functions where we were expected to present ourselves a certain way. My mother loves all that comes with the rich life. She spends her days shopping and meeting her lunch club friends.

I grab the first dress I see in a small boutique. It's the second shop we've been in, and Penelope gives me one of her disapproving looks. "It's nice," I argue, holding it up.

"It is nice, but you're just rushing it. You should look at some others first."

"I don't need to. I've found this one." I take it to the counter, and the young sales lady looks at the dress and then at me.

"Will you be trying it on first?" she asks, arching her brow.

"No, it's exactly my size," I bite back, rolling my eyes, and Penelope glares at me.

"Try the dress on, Lucy," she hisses, taking it from the counter and marching over to the fitting room. I huff like a sulky teenager and stomp after her.

I was right, the dress fits me perfectly. The black material clings to my curves, and with the right bra, my breasts will look amazing spilling over the top. It runs down to my ankles and then fans out in a fishtail style. Penelope steps back and looks me up and down. "Actually, it looks amazing," she says with a smile.

"I told you. I always look great in cocktail dresses," I say, spinning slowly and checking the back in the mirror.

I place the dress on the counter again and smile smugly. "Fits like a glove," I say, and the woman returns a tight smile.

"Fantastic. I'll just wrap that for you."

When I finally step into the apartment, I'm not surprised to see it's full of flowers. Vases on every surface are full of pink lilies, my favourite flower. Noah appears from the bedroom, his face forlorn and full of regret. "I didn't think you'd ever come home," he mutters.

"I thought you were at work all day," I say, noting that it's only just past noon.

"I came home early, hoping you'd be here so I could apologise for my atrocious behaviour last night." I watch him walk towards me. It's the same story. He does this at least once a month, and the apology is always the same. I genuinely think that he is sorry. If I didn't, I wouldn't still be here. I just wish he would remember this moment and stop getting so drunk. "I don't deserve you, baby. I'm a bastard, but please forgive me." He gently rubs his thumb over my bruised cheek. "I can't believe I did that to you," he adds.

"It's fine. It's done now. You didn't have to buy me all these flowers."

"You deserve so much more." He pulls a jewellery box from his back pocket and opens it. A beautiful sapphire ring sits in the box. It'll go lovely with the other beautiful jewellery he's bought me out of guilt. He doesn't notice that I don't wear any of it, though I guess he doesn't really care once I've accepted the apology. I smile awkwardly, hating expensive gift. I place a gentle kiss on his cheek.

"Thank you, I love it." I know what's coming next when he leans in for a longer kiss. The last thing I want to do is have sex with Noah, but it's kind of a requirement when he buys me jewellery that I don't want. He takes my hand and leads me towards the bedroom. Noah is very traditional, preferring missionary sex in our bed.

I place the ring beside the bed, vowing to add it to the others in the safe. We strip off in silence and climb into bed. Noah props himself up on one elbow and lies on his side. He pulls the sheet from my body and stares at me for a few seconds, then he runs his hand along my side until he reaches my breast. Leaning forward, he runs his tongue across my nipple and then sucks it into his mouth. There's nothing romantic about it, and I resist the urge to shudder. I let him do his thing, laying silently while he licks and sucks parts of my body.

When he's ready, he climbs between my legs and prods my opening with his erection. "Are you ready, baby?" he whispers. I smile up at him and nod. Noah lunges forward, and I suck in a surprised breath. Usually, he's much more gentle. He smirks down at me, thinking I'm enjoying this. He pumps in and out no more than five times, and then he shudders, groaning in my ear as he releases into me.

Once he's caught his breath, he places a kiss against my lips. "I love you," he whispers.

"I love you too." I smile, and just like that, our argument is forgotten.

TAG

I take the drink from the tray Ella holds out for me. She's bent low enough for me to look down her top, and when she catches me staring, she smirks. "Thank you, Ella," her father, Conner, mutters, eyeing the two of us suspiciously. "There's been no sightings of your father?" he asks. I know he thinks something is going on, like my useless, drunk arse father and I have conspired to get him out of the country so that he doesn't have to answer to Conner.

"No, sir. I've got men everywhere looking for him. I don't want to spend too much manpower on it. I'm getting bored," I say, keeping my tone even. Conner is the only man I know who can look at you and know you're lying before you've even told the lie. The truth being that I have hardly any men out looking because I don't care. The longer he stays away, the more chance I have of stepping into his shoes, and then

Conner Martinez will be more inclined to let me marry his goddess of a daughter.

My father is an important man in our world. Our family name causes fear in the men amongst us, as does Conner's, who heads all our families. There's a hierarchy—Conner is at the top of the chain, followed by my father, or me because he's currently missing, and then it branches off into families that work for us. Some have more of our respect than others, but generally, they all answer to my father, and then he answers to Conner. We bring money in from the London streets, providing a protection racket for the bars and clubs in our area. They pay us to keep their properties and everyone inside of them safe, and we do a great job. That's one of the reasons I'm here today, to hand over Conner's cut for the week, something my father would do if he wasn't AWOL right now.

"What are your plans once you find him?" he asks, placing a cigar into his mouth and lighting the thick end.

"Whatever is expected of me," I say, my eyes catching Ella's as she enters the room again, her kitten curled up against her chest. How I wish that was me.

Anton kicks my foot, bringing my attention back to Conner. "You know you have to find him, Tag. Once I have spoken to him, he will be executed. There can be no negotiation." I nod once in understanding. If I get the chance, I'll put the bullet in him myself. He may have brought shame on me and my mother, but I won't let him be tortured to death. He doesn't deserve that.

Conner stands. "I have an appointment to get to. I'll speak with the families tomorrow. I think you should step up as head of your family. I don't see why we should wait." I bow my head as a sign of respect since he wouldn't appreciate me shouting 'hell yeah'. "They may need to see more from you, Tag. Not just in the cage."

He leaves the room, kissing his daughter on the head as he passes her. Anton turns to me, grinning from ear to ear. "Finally."

"About time, you mean," I mutter.

Ella takes the seat that her father vacated. She makes a show of crossing her slender, tanned legs, still holding the grey kitten to her chest. "A boss," she says, her glossy lips almost breaking a smile. I know she's thinking the same as me, even if she is playing it cool in front of her brother.

Anton rises to his feet. "I'll go get changed. We'll head out for training and then get food?" I nod, and he leaves me alone with Ella. I crook my finger, and she arches her brow. She likes to defy me, a game I love.

"El," I mutter, my voice low with a warning tone. She smirks and places the kitten on the floor. Her skirt is way too short, something she won't get away with when she's mine. I wait until she's in front of me, then I take her fingers in my hand and give her a gentle tug so she falls onto my lap.

She laughs. "Really, Tag, here?"

"You know me, I like to live dangerously." She places her hand against my stubbly cheek and then licks her tongue across my lower lip. "Will you be at the fight tomorrow night?" I ask.

She shrugs, placing gentle kisses along my chin until she gets back to my lips, and then she kisses me with such passion that I curl my toes. I run my hand along her ribs, but before I can reach her breast, she halts me, removing my hand and placing it onto the couch beside me. She smiles against my mouth when I groan in frustration. It's a game she plays continuously, but in our families, the girls respect themselves enough to wait until marriage for sex. She presses her arse against my erection. "Soon, Boss, soon."

I hear Anton's footfalls on the stairs, and I grip her hips and stand her up. She wipes around her glossy lips and then picks up the kitten, moving away from me and running her hand along the bookshelf, pretending she's looking for her next read. "Right, brother, let's go," he says.

Chapter Four

♥

LUCY

I smile politely at the large, suited man standing before me ogling my breasts. "So, Colin, tell me how you won that Brown case, because we had bets it wouldn't go your way," says Noah, handing me a fresh glass of Champagne and removing my half-full one. He doesn't think Champagne should ever be drunk at room temperature, which I think is ridiculous and wasteful. He places my old glass on a passing waitress's tray.

"You have no faith, Noah," scoffs Colin, his raucous laugh catching the attention of the surrounding people. A passing man catches Colin's eye, and he turns to speak with him.

"Are you having a nice evening?" asks Noah, tucking my hair behind my ear.

I untuck it and smile. "Of course." He places a light kiss on my lips, but feeling daring, and possibly tipsy, I try to take it deeper.

Noah pulls back slightly, a confused grimace on his face. "Are you okay?"

I run my hand up his shirt, laying it against his chest. "Maybe we could slip off. There are lots of dark corners where we could spend a few minutes alone." I smile, adding a wink.

Noah laughs awkwardly, kissing me lightly on the nose. "You are so cute, baby," he says, and then he turns to the couple behind us and introduces himself. I roll my eyes. I'd half expected him to ruffle my hair at the end of that brush off.

"Having fun, darling?" Charlotte Fielding's irritating voice almost makes me shudder. I turn to watch her approaching form glide towards me and I'd swear she floats just like a witch. She air-kisses my cheeks and then repeats her son's action and tucks my hair behind my ear.

"I'm having the best time," I lie, untucking my hair and running my fingers through it to shake the bouncy curls out.

"Sarcasm really is a low form of wit, dear," she mutters.

"Is Clyde not here yet?" I ask, knowing full well that he is. I'd seen him sneak off ten minutes ago with a sexy blonde.

"He's somewhere around here. We arrived separate because he came straight from work." She cranes her neck to look around the room.

"I'm just going to powder my nose. Please let Noah know where I am when he's finished talking," I say, and then I push through the crowds to where the restroom sign lights up brightly.

I push the door, and despite there being numerous toilets inside, there's a line of around ten women. I sigh and decide to go and look for one farther afield. I step out of the grand room into the large entrance hall, where the odd waiter is waiting with their Champagne bottles to refill the waitresses' trays. "Excuse me," I say politely to one. He looks up and his expression is cold. I get it, he thinks this pompous event is full of stuck-up arseholes, and he'd be right, but I'm not one of them. "Is there another bathroom? I one in there is full," I say.

He points to another door across the room but doesn't speak. *Rude.* I huff and then make my way in the direction he pointed. There's a winding staircase, and I wonder why the bathroom is always up the damn stairs. Once I reach the top, I freeze, not wanting to make a sound. I debate whether to just turn around and leave or run straight into the bathroom, which is literally two steps to my left. Noah's father is at the far end of the corridor with the blonde's legs wrapped around his waist, and he's thrusting hard and fast.

"Lucy, did you find the bathroom? The one downstairs is full." I spin around at the sound of Charlotte's voice as she climbs the stairs elegantly. Clyde freezes and looks over his shoulder, panic in his eyes as they meet mine. My instinct takes over, and I turn and march down the stairs towards Charlotte.

"Would you believe it's out of order? Honestly, all this expense and not one free toilet. We should complain." I link my arm with hers, and we head back towards the ball room.

I'm saved as we re-enter the ballroom because Penelope has arrived. She gives me a slight wave, and I release Charlotte's arm so she can go off and mingle. "Thank god you're here." I sigh, air-kissing her. "Where's Wyatt?"

"He's been dragged off to talk business," she says, rolling her eyes. "Noah?"

"Same. I hate these things. I'm so bored." I sigh, taking a glass of Champagne from a passing waitress. "And I really hate this stuff." I huff, taking a sip of the bubbly liquid.

"We all do, darling. Just hold the glass for show like I do," she says, smiling at a passing couple. "It's almost time to be seated. Shall we go and check the seating plan?"

My phone vibrates and I fish it out of my clutch. Tyra has sent me a photograph of herself and Maribel making silly faces at the camera. I smile and then send a text off asking what they're up to. She wastes no time in replying, asking how my boring party is and telling me they're in a wine bar in central London. I'm so jealous, and even more so when we check the table plan and I realise I'm sitting at a table without Penelope.

I go to my seat and find Noah is already at the table. To his left sits the blonde who was with Clyde earlier. They're deep in conversation and hardly notice as I take the seat to Noah's right. I sit in silence for at least five minutes before Noah's parents join us. We stand to greet them, even though I've already air-kissed Charlotte once. I watch Clyde closely as he kisses the blonde on her cheek and then he turns to Charlotte. "Darling, this is Emma. She's been a godsend to the firm." I arch a brow, and Clyde avoids making eye contact with me.

Charlotte smiles, taking Emma's hand and shaking it gently. "Clyde and Noah have told me so much about you."

I fold my arms across my chest. Noah hasn't ever mentioned this woman before, and it doesn't look like anyone is going to introduce me as they all begin to take their seats again. I lean across the table, holding out my hand. "I'm Lucy, Noah's fiancée." She takes my hand, her eyes casually darting between Noah and Clyde.

"My girlfriend," corrects Noah, and I glare at him. How dare he correct me like that in front of this perfectly groomed female? He gives a small chuckle and runs a hand over my shoulder.

"Noah hasn't mentioned you. Have you worked for him long?" I ask, choosing to ignore Noah's comment.

Emma smiles sweetly. "Three months."

"Wow, quite some time for him not to mention you then," I say, glancing to Noah, who is now settled back into his chair. "And you're a secretary?" I ask, because clearly no one here is going to tell me.

"Gosh, no," she giggles, "Noah is my mentor. He's training me to be as amazing as he is."

"You're a lawyer?" I almost screech because she looks about eighteen. "Are you old enough for that?"

"Lucy," admonishes Charlotte. She's big on manners unless she's the one being rude.

"I mean, you look so young," I explain.

"I get my genes from my mother's side, I'm twenty-two." That's at least thirty years between her and Clyde, I shudder.

"Have you finished with the Spanish Inquisition now?" asks Noah. I'll save the Spanish Inquisition for him later because I find it odd that he hasn't mentioned Emma when he's clearly spending a lot of time with her.

TAG

I wipe my mouth on the napkin. The meal was amazing, but I'd have preferred the company of Ella over her brother. "Where to next?" asks Anton. I shrug, because honestly, I can't get Ella off my mind today. The fact that I could be made head of the Corallo family permanently means I'm a step closer to getting exactly what I want... her. "Are you okay? You seem a little distant tonight."

I sigh. "Thinking about my father."

"Let's hope he's taken our advice and stays away. The minute he's back here, he'll be killed."

"He won't come back. With all that money, he won't need to." The last insult was my father stealing money from the families. We discovered he'd been skimming money for some time, so who knows how much he's saved. When Anton and I figured it out, he admitted it. We should have killed him, but at the end of the day, he's still my father, so we let him run on the condition that he never return. If he comes back here, I won't let him run again. I can't afford to look weak once I'm head of my family.

"I think we should go to a club, find some girls, and have a party. You still have some catching up to do," teases Anton, "after number ten blew you off last night, not literally, of course." He laughs at his own joke.

"I was thinking about that. Let's raise the stakes," I say, chucking some cash on the table to cover the meal. "Ten was a bitch. She called me smooth, and not in a good way. I want to teach her a lesson and win at the same time." Anton looks at me with interest as he follows me from the restaurant. He loves a good game. "If I get Ten into my bed, then you have to support me when I make a claim for your sister. Your father is more likely to accept it if you're on my side." It's not a secret between us that I love his sister, I have for many years, but he knows me too well and he knows what I'm like when it comes to girls and sex. I'm the last person he wants Ella to marry.

"Ten would never go for you. She's shown you no interest."

"Then what have you got to lose?"

He ponders it for a moment. "We know nothing about Ten. How would you find her?"

"Her friend is a journalist for *The London Gazette*. I'll start there."

"Okay, if I go along with this, what do I get out of it when you lose?"

"What do you want?" I ask.

We turn the corner, cross the busy road, and head straight for the door of Breach, a popular nightclub owned by Anton's family. There's a long queue outside, but one of the three doormen lifts the thick red rope for us and we go inside. "I want something big if I'm agreeing to you and my sister. Not that it'll ever happen because Ten will not sleep with you."

"Let me worry about that."

"Okay, I want your apartment." I spin to look at him. I love my apartment, and he knows how much I love it because not only did it cost me a ridiculous amount to buy outright, but it's in a nice part of London, in Chelsea. It overlooks the River Thames, and it's in a highly sought-after area. I had to wait almost two years for something to become available.

"My apartment?" I almost yell. "Are you shitting me?"

"Man, you want my sister," he yells back, laughing. "And it can't just be as simple as you getting number ten into bed. It needs to be bigger than that."

"Bigger?"

"Yeah," he taps his chin like he's thinking hard, "make her fall in love with you."

"Don't be ridiculous. Ten has a boyfriend. Making her fall in love with me is a little farfetched."

"Well, that's the deal, man, take it or leave it."

We step into the VIP area. It's full of hot women and important men. We move through the room, stopping to shake hands occasionally as we pass people we know. I fist bump with Cruise. "Ah, just the man I was looking for," I say, slapping him on the back.

"What can I do for you, Tag?"

"I need help finding someone. Female, works for *London Gazette*. She's black, gorgeous-looking, and I'm pretty sure her name is something like Tyler. It's actually her friend I'm after, but all I have on her is her name, which is Lucy."

"Leave it with me, man, I'll look into it." We shake hands, and he disappears into the crowd as I slide into the booth next to Anton. We're joined by a few other guys, all around our age and all sons of important families.

Anton is filling them in on the details of next week's fight. I join in the conversation, but my mind is on hatching a plan, one that has me keeping my apartment and winning Ella. As if my mind conjures her up, I spot Ella entering the VIP room. Her skin-tight pants have my eyes bulging from my head, and her midriff is on display because her top is practically a bra. I nudge Anton, and he follows my stare.

"What the fuck?" he growls. We both march towards her, and she rolls her eyes. "Seriously, Ella, what are you doing here?"

"I'm out for Tiffany's birthday. Daddy cleared it," she says with a shrug.

"Does he know you came out in your underwear?" growls Anton.

She sighs. "It's what all the girls wear, Ant. Don't start."

"But not the daughter of Conner Martinez," I say firmly. "Have some fucking self-respect." Ella turns her hurt eyes to me. I don't want other men looking at her skin, but I can't tell her that, not in front of Anton and not until she's mine.

"You two want to lecture me about self-respect when you sleep with girls for a stupid game?"

"Go home, Ella," commands Anton. He indicates for his driver, who is standing by the exit. "Take Ella home, please."

"For God's sake," she yells. "I'm not a kid, Anton. I don't have to do what you say!"

Anton grips her by the arm and yanks her closer to him. I grit my teeth because every fibre of my being wants to rip his hand from her skin. "You'll do as you're fucking told," he growls.

Ella pulls her arm free and rubs at the large red mark on her pale skin. "I hate you." She stomps away with Anton's driver following.

Cruise is standing by my table when I return. "Boss, I have some good news." He smiles. "The journalist is Tyra James-Banks and she's in this club tonight."

I grin wide, patting him on the back. "That was quick work," I point out.

"I know someone who works on *The Gazette*. Then I tracked her phone, and she pinged up in here. I've sent security to invite her into the VIP area."

"You amaze me, Cruise, you fucking genius."

I relay the information to Anton, who smirks. "So, the plan is to what exactly?"

"I'm gonna do some homework on Ten and then make my decision on our little bet."

Anton shakes his head, laughing, "No way. That's not how this works. You made the bet, either take it now or forget it."

Tyra is led into the VIP lounge, along with another friend who was also there last night, but there's no sign of Ten, which disappoints me. *How hard can it be? I've slept with hundreds of women, and it's never been an issue getting them to fall for me.* I hold my hand out to Anton, and he smiles, gripping it in his. We shake on it and the deal is set. Now, I need a plan.

Chapter Five

LUCY

Tyra: Oh my god, Luce, you will never guess where we are. In the VIP lounge in Breach!!!!!

I re-read the text. Looking around the huge room, surrounded by important people from the business world, I sigh. I would much rather be at Breach with the girls. I drum my polished fingernails on the table, and Noah shoots me an annoyed look. He's spent the entire evening so far chatting with his new prodigy, Emma, while I'm stuck listening to his parents bickering about where they want to go on their holiday next month.

My phone flashes again. This time, it's a photo of that prick from last night, Tag. He doesn't know she's taken it. He looks deep in conversation, and it's been taken from a distance.

Me: Stop stalking him, you crazy bitch!

Tyra: I'm gonna stalk that beast right into bed seeing as you wasted the chance. I'll let you know how big he is.

Her message is followed by a winking emoji. I shake my head and laugh, stuffing my phone back into my clutch bag. She'd be crazy to go anywhere near that creep—he's more than likely riddled with STDs.

I lean in towards Noah and whisper, "When can we go?"

"After the awards," he says, and I groan. That's going to be another couple of hours at least. They haven't even begun yet, and the meal has only just finished.

"Well, could you at least talk to me? I'm sitting here listening to your mother moan about holidays to France."

"I'm trying to make Emma feel comfortable. She's up for best newcomer," he says.

"They have best newcomer to business?" I smirk. "What do you have to do to get that award, show up for work every day?"

Noah scowls. "I know you don't take all of this very seriously, but the rest of us here do."

"It's not that I don't take it seriously, I do, I just think it's weird having an award for best newcomer. Anyway, why haven't you mentioned her before?"

"Because you don't listen when I talk about work. Do I need to start reeling off a list of people I work with?"

"No, just the ones you're mentoring, especially when they look like Emma," I whisper-hiss.

Noah rolls his eyes. "You're being ridiculous. Is it any wonder I'm sitting here talking to Emma when you're behaving like a child?" He turns back to Emma, and I sigh. I look to where Penelope is sitting just three tables over. There's a vacant seat next to her, so I make a dash over to her.

"Can I sit here for a minute? My table is so boring," I whisper.

"Please do," she whispers back. "I think the woman who was sitting here left. She said she was bored, and I've actually debated following her. Wyatt has spent most of the time wandering amongst the tables talking to other people. He didn't bother to eat half his food."

"Noah's spent most of the night talking to Emma," I mutter, glancing back to where he's still animatedly chatting to her.

"Who's Emma?"

"Apparently, Noah is mentoring her, not that he ever mentioned her at all. Don't you think that's weird?"

Penelope shrugs. "Not really. If he spoke of her all the time, you'd be suspicious."

"Well, I don't like her, and I certainly don't trust her."

"Is she pretty?" asks Penelope, arching her brow.

"Well, yes, but that's not why I don't like her. Earlier, I was looking for another bathroom and I saw Clyde and her fucking against the wall upstairs. It was very awkward."

Penelope's mouth drops open. She loves gossip. "Oh my goodness, did he see you?"

"Well, not at first, but then Charlotte made an appearance, and he heard her voice. Of course, I saved the day and marched her back downstairs. But then I find out that Emma's working so closely with Noah, and I can't help but wonder if she's just trying to make it to the top by sleeping her way through the partners."

"Sweetie, no one would sleep with Clyde just to make it to the top. Maybe she wants his money?" It's a more likely scenario. He is very rich, but then so is Noah. Clyde isn't the best looking of men. His face is tired and ruddy, and although he likes to keep fit by running every day, he's still rounded in the middle.

"Is Wyatt up for any awards?" I ask, not really caring either way. Why do the people in this room care about stupid contributions to business awards when they're so rich and busy?

"No, but his firm might be. The whole thing is pointless, just an excuse for rich arseholes to get together and talk about how great and powerful they are."

"We could always sneak out. Tyra and Maribel are at a club. They got into the VIP lounge and it looks pretty amazing."

"I'm sure Tyra would love to see me there," says Penelope dryly, and I laugh. I love all my friends, but it's no secret that they aren't so keen on each other. Tyra hates what she likes to call 'my people'. She thinks they're all stuck up and show-offs. It's not entirely true. I think Penelope gets nervous around Tyra and so she sometimes blabbers away about money and holidays just to fill the silence. I try to keep the groups separate. Things I do with Bel and Tyra, like going to cage fights and nightclubs, are not the sort of things I do with Penelope, Gabriella, and Francesca. With them, I go for dinner and the theatre.

"Well, I'm going to the bathroom, seeing as the last time, I got distracted."

This time, the bathroom is completely free. It's beautiful inside, with one of those large areas in the centre of the room that looks more like a living room than a bathroom. There are leather couches and huge vases of flowers. Once I've finished, I wash my hands and check my makeup in the mirror. Penelope's makeup girl was amazing—you can't see a single bruise.

"Noah tells me you have the cutest job." Emma approaches me as I watch her through the reflection of the mirror. She reminds me of a panther about to make her first kill.

"Did he?"

"Hmm, you throw parties or something like that?" She pretends to think for a second, "My three-year-old niece has a birthday coming up. Shall I pass on your business card to my sister?"

"Actually, I plan weddings mostly," I say, wiping away the stray mascara underneath one eye. "High-end weddings," I add.

"Oh, so you're a wedding planner, like in the film with Jennifer Lopez?"

"Tell me, Emily," I say, purposely getting her name wrong, "are you married yet?"

Emma guffaws. "Gosh, no."

"Pity. It's always nice to have your own husband rather than stealing someone else's, especially in your line of work. People might get the wrong idea."

"What are you talking about?" she snaps, narrowing her eyes.

"I'm just saying, you wouldn't want people thinking that you slept your way to the top." I pick up my purse and saunter towards the door. "Does Noah know you're fucking his father?" I throw over my shoulder as the door closes behind me.

TAG

I take the bottle of beer from the bartender and nudge my arm against Tyra's. I purposely stood here so I could start a natural conversation with her. "Sorry," I say, smiling wide. She smooths her black hair and flutters her long lashes in my direction.

"No problem." She smiles, flashing her perfectly straight white teeth. If I wasn't interested in her friend, I might be tempted to try it on with Tyra.

"I've met you before?" I ask, cocking my head to one side like I'm trying to work out where I've seen her. "Do you work at my gym?"

Tyra shakes her head. "No, I saw your fight. Well done, by the way."

"That's right, you came back for the afterparty with your friends." Delighted that I remember her, she nods and takes a sip of her drink.

"Tag Corallo, by the way," I say, holding out my hand.

She shakes it. "Tyra James-Banks," she says, "and this is my friend, Maribel."

"Why don't you come over and join me?" I add, pointing towards my booth. She ponders it for a moment and then smiles before grabbing her friend's hand and following me.

Some of the guys shuffle around, making room for the girls. I introduce them to everyone and then settle opposite them. "At the afterparty, you had another friend with you."

"Yeah, that's right, Lucy."

"She not with you tonight?" I ask, looking around the crowd.

"No, she had a thing tonight with her boyfriend," says Tyra. "Some posh awards thing."

"Posh?" I repeat. She didn't seem the type to attend awards ceremonies. "Is she getting an award?"

"No, her boyfriend probably is, or his stupid company." Neither of Lucy's friends look impressed by this.

"You don't like him?" I ask with a laugh.

"Not really. Lucy can do better," mutters Bel. That's exactly what I want to hear. If I play this right, I'll have her friends' support and then I've practically got this in the bag.

"But she doesn't agree?" I ask, taking a wild guess.

Tyra sighs. "Nobody ever thinks they're with the wrong person until they're free of them."

"So, what makes this guy so wrong for your friend?" I ask, and they both stare at me sceptically. "I'm interested. This stuff helps a guy in future relationships," I joke, and they both smile and relax.

"He just doesn't treat her nice. Makes backhanded comments about what she wears or how she behaves. I mean, Lucy is no pushover, but he's just mean to her. It's like he thinks he's too good for her."

"To be honest, I spoke to your friend that night, and she wasn't exactly miss friendly," I point out.

"She's prickly," Tyra shrugs, "but she's lovely. You should see how creative she is. Her work is amazing."

"She's an artist?" I ask in surprise, and she laughs again, shaking her head.

"No, a wedding planner. High-end weddings mostly, but my god can that girl throw the best party," says Tyra. "In fact, if you're getting married any time soon, you should call her."

I lean forward slightly. "You never know when that could come in handy. Where is she based? I have a few friends who are getting married, maybe I can send them her way."

Tyra fiddles around in her purse for a moment and then smiles triumphantly, handing me a buff business card. I glance down at the address, it's just a short walk from my gym. I smile and tuck it inside my pocket. This was going to be so much easier than I thought.

Monday rolls around, and I get into my running gear and spend the first hour of my day pounding the streets. Conner is waiting for me at my apartment when I get home, and I wipe my hand on my hooded top before shaking his. "What brings you here so early?" I ask as I unlock the apartment door and we head inside.

"I came to tell you that your father is officially out of the family. The other families agreed that you will be the head of the Corallo family." I keep my back to him while I fish about in the fridge for a bottled water. This was all agreed too easy, I wasn't expecting it. "Of course, there's one condition," he adds. "For you to be head of the family, the original head needs to be deceased. We expect news of your father's death by the end of the month."

I spin to face him. "But that's three weeks away," I say. "I don't even know where the hell he is, Conner."

He scowls at me. "Be careful, Tag. Remember who I am."

I bow my head in respect. It's not acceptable to shoot your mouth off to the head of the Mafia, even though he's known me most of my life. "Sorry, boss. I'm surprised is all."

"It's time to grow up now, Tag. Being head of your family is going to be a big responsibility. You need to step up your security because we'll be making the official announcement within the week. I thought I'd pay your mother a visit first. I don't suppose she'll be too happy with the decision."

Conner's right. My mother begged me not to step up, but it isn't quite that simple. It would have gone to my uncle, who's a total arse, and he would have ruined our family name and probably gotten us all killed with his bad decision-making.

Once Conner leaves, I give Antonio a call. He's part of my security team at the moment, not that I feel I need any security. I am an MMA fighter after all. But if Conner's told me to increase security, that's what I need to do. I advise Antonio that we need two more men and leave him to hire them. He's been around for the last five years, and I trust him with my life.

I shower and then spend some time catching up on emails. My mother helps runs one of our family businesses, a jewellery store in central London. We cater to a higher end market, and there's a few emails about meetings this week with suppliers. I forward them onto my mother as a reminder and warn her that Conner is on his way to see her.

Dressing in a dark blue Armani suit, I text Dan, my driver, to get the car ready. I have a certain number ten that I want to see.

The car slows down outside Lucy's shop. It's bright, just like I imagined it to be. The white walls make it stand out amongst the other brick buildings, and her windows are full of balloons and other wedding paraphernalia. There's no parking around this part of London, so I tell Dan to drive around until I call him. Taking a deep breath, I open the shop door and step inside.

It's sleek inside, less shop-like and more office. There are two desks towards the back of the room where a man is currently chatting on the telephone. He looks up as I enter and holds a finger up to tell me he'll be a minute. I nod and begin to flick through a large book laying open on top of a glass cabinet. Inside are various photos of number ten in different wedding dresses. She's stunning, and this is the only time I've ever been attracted to a woman in a wedding dress.

The man ends the call and then stands. "Sorry about that. How can I help you?"

"I'm actually looking for the owner," I say as we shake hands.

"Lucy? She'll be back any minute. She loves her pastries first thing, and she's a cow without her sugar fix. Oh, speak of the devil," he says, nodding towards the door as Lucy walks in with her back to us. She manoeuvres through the door with a coffee in each hand and a brown paper bag hanging from her mouth. She makes some inaudible sounds, and the man rushes to help her, taking the coffees.

She removes the paper bag from her mouth. "I mean honestly, some people are just rude," she rants, then she turns to face me and freezes. "Oh," she mumbles, "it's you."

"Number ten, fancy seeing you here," I say, adding a lopsided smile.

Chapter Six

LUCY

My heart hammers in my chest. It's hard not to react to the gorgeous hunk of a man standing before me. He looks good in a suit, the navy colour bringing out the blue in his eyes and enhancing his tanned skin. "Are you here to book our services?" I ask, cocking an eyebrow. I seriously doubt this guy is the type to get married, and if he is, then I feel sorry for his poor fiancée.

"Maybe. How good are you?"

"I've never had a dissatisfied customer yet," I say.

"I can imagine you to be meticulous with every detail." He talks like that's a bad thing. "Almost anal."

"Details are extremely important when arranging a wedding." Keelan is staring between us with confusion. "Keelan, this is Tag. Remember, the arsehole I told you about."

"Ohhhh," grins Keelan, "the fighter."

"Come for a drink with me," Tag finally says. "Please."

"No," I say firmly, but inside, my inner girl is screaming 'yes'.

"Why?"

"Because I don't want to."

"But that's impossible. I mean, it's never happened to me before and I don't know how to handle it." His tone is mocking, and I almost give in and smile.

"Wow," I laugh, "you've seriously never been told no, have you?"

"Nope, only by my mother, if she counts."

I sit behind my desk and open my laptop. I'm playing it cool, but my inner girl is kicking me for saying no. "You can leave now, I'm busy."

"I'm not leaving until you agree to a drink with me. I feel like we got off to a bad start, Ten. I want to clear the air."

"How did you know I would be here?"

"Say yes," he repeats.

"I'm not going out with you." I sigh when he takes a seat opposite me and folds his arms over his chest. His sleeves ride up, revealing tattoos on both arms.

"Lucy, go for a coffee with the guy. Stop being a bore," says Keelan, and I glare in his direction. He's such a softy for a sob story. "I'll cover Miss Grey's appointment."

"No, she'll be upset if she thinks I've deserted her."

"Don't be ridiculous, the guy wants to say sorry." Tag is nodding in agreement, and I roll my eyes.

"I'm meeting Noah for lunch," I say, and Keelan screws his face up. He's another hater of my boyfriend.

"I'll have you back within half an hour. It's hours until lunch," promises Tag.

"One coffee." I groan, and my inner girl whoops and cheers as I scrape my chair back like a sulky teenager.

We step out onto the busy street. It's rush hour and people are darting in and out of the crowds, making their way to work. Tag grabs hold of my hand and, before I can protest, he pulls me across the street towards a small coffee shop. Once inside, I pull my hand free. "You get a seat, and I'll get the coffee," he says.

Tag brings me a latte, and as he slides into his seat, I marvel at how huge he looks in this tiny shop. "So," he smiles, "I'm Matteo Corallo." He holds out his hand, I take it, and we shake.

"I'm Lucy Clifford."

"Lovely to meet you, Lucy, although 'number ten' has kind of stuck. I might keep calling you that."

"What is the number thing all about?" I ask, sipping on my latte.

"Nothing important. It's simply a way to keep an eye on numbers. If we over-invite, things can get messy." He shrugs, but I don't buy it.

"Or it's a way to remember girls—numbers instead of names," I suggest, and he laughs.

"No, really, it's nothing more than crowd control."

"When's your next fight?"

"This weekend. Just a money-maker, nothing big like the last one. Why don't you come?"

"It's not really my thing," I mutter.

"Yeah, your friend said you weren't the partying kind."

I stare for a moment. Why would Tyra say something like that? I knew it wouldn't be Bel because she wouldn't bitch about me like that. "I love a good party. I just don't care for violence."

"Oh, then you'll definitely hate this weekend. I'm fighting a gypsy king, and they tend to make things messy."

"What else do you do, apart from fight?"

"I have businesses, a jeweller among other things, all family owned and run."

"So, why fight if you have an income?"

"Because I love it. I was born to fight. My father used to say I had a rage inside of me from the second I was born. It only seems to calm when I've fought. Who knows what I'd become without that."

"Does your father fight?"

"My father's dead," he says. It's blunt and stony, like he doesn't want to discuss it.

"Oh, sorry, I didn't realise."

"Why would you? You don't know me... yet."

An awkward silence falls between us. "Why do they call you Tag?"

"It's just a stage name, but it stuck and now everyone calls me that. Only my mother calls me Matteo. She's American, moved here years ago and met my father. He came up with the name, saying it stood for The Angry Gangster." We laugh and then fall silent again. I feel a strange pull to him, and I wonder if he feels it too. His cocky attitude is making me think naughty thoughts rather than repulsing me, and I start to question what the hell is going on with me. I shift in my seat and then glance out of the window just in time to see Noah entering my shop across the street. I stand abruptly, my chair hitting the customer sitting behind me.

"Oh shit, I have to go. Sorry, Tag, it was nice to see you again." He follows me from the cafe, firing questions about my sudden departure. As I get to the door of my shop, Noah is coming back out. He scowls when he sees Tag.

"I came to cancel lunch, but I see you're occupied," he says coldly.

I glance back to Tag and then smile at Noah. "Oh, this is just Tag. He's thinking of hiring me for his wedding to . . ." I trail off, and Tag steps forward.

"To Ella," he says, and I breathe a sigh of relief.

"Right," says Noah, eyeing us suspiciously. "Well, I have a lunch appointment with Emma that I forgot about. I'll also be home late, if

I even make it at all. We have a huge case to start working on, so we might pull an all-nighter." He takes my hand and strokes it with his thumb. "Sorry, Boo."

I hide my disappointment. These late nights and business lunches are becoming too regular. "Not to worry. I'll find something to keep me busy."

He kisses me on the forehead and smiles down at me. "Maybe you can work on Taylor's little wedding. You like a good project."

I nod, his condescending tone pissing me off, but I don't bother to correct his mistake. "Have a good night." I watch him saunter back down the road to his office. *Arse.*

Tag follows me into the shop. "Well, I see why none of your friends like him."

"Who said they didn't like him?" I snap.

Keelan keeps his head down and stares intently at his computer screen like he's suddenly busy. "Tyra and Bel," Tag says.

"Whatever. They're both single, so their opinions don't count. Who's Ella?" I add.

"Jealous?" he asks, and I glare. *As if.* "Who even kisses a girl on the head like that, unless they're eighty?" I hear Keelan snort. "What time do you close up?"

"None of your business."

"Around four," says Keelan.

"I'll pick you up. What size are you? I'll bring you some gym gear."

"What?" I almost screech, but he's out the door before I can protest.

"Oh my god, you didn't say he was so hot," snaps Keelan, fanning himself.

"You think every man over five-foot is hot, especially if he has tattoos."

"And you turned him down. What the hell is wrong with you?"

"I'm in a relationship," I remind him.

TAG

I drive to Anton's with a smile on my face. When I arrive, he's outside with his huge black Doberman. He's training the crazy dog, but he'd have more luck training a lion than that unruly beast. I step from my car and lean back against it, folding my arms across my chest. "Is Ella around?"

"Why? You haven't won the bet yet."

I snort a laugh because we both know I will. "I need to borrow some gym gear from her. I'm taking Ten on a date."

Anton looks up sharply. "What? How the hell did you manage that?"

"It's my good looks and charm." I wink as I pass him and head inside.

I take the stairs two at a time until I reach the second floor. Ella's room is at the end of the hall—I know because I've managed to sneak in there a few times—and I tap lightly on the door before walking in. Ella is laying on her stomach, kicking her feet against her arse as she looks down at a textbook. She's always got her nose in a book studying, and I love that about her. She smiles at me and drops the pen she was chewing on. "Hey, does Ant know you're in here?"

I throw myself onto her bed so that I'm lying beside her. "Do you care?"

"Yes, he'll make my life hell."

I slap her perky backside, and she hisses. I can't wait to show her all the things I've been fantasising about for the last few years. "Kiss me," I mutter, rolling onto my back.

Ella kisses me on the cheek, and I groan with frustration. She giggles before leaning in for a deeper kiss. I push my hand under her stomach and then lift her so that she rolls on top of me. Her legs fall to either side of my hips and she places her hands on my chest for balance. Her tongue sweeps into my mouth, and I squeeze her thighs gently. She pushes herself to sit up, still astride me. She must feel the hardness in my pants, but she doesn't say anything. Instead, she blushes, and I love how innocent she is.

"I've made a deal with your brother," I say quietly. "We have a kind of bet going. If I win, he has to back me up when it comes to me claiming you. Your father is more likely to accept it with Anton's backing."

"And if you lose?"

"I won't," I say with confidence. "I'm gonna buy you a huge house. We're gonna have babies. I can't wait to see you pregnant." I grin, and she laughs.

"All you think about is sex," she says. I take her hands in mine, locking our fingers and then placing them above my head so she has to lean closer to me. I steal another kiss and wriggle beneath her so that my erection rubs against her. Her face flushes further, and I keep moving, the denim of my jeans causing enough friction to make her breathless. She pants, and I release one of her hands so I can grope her breast through her top. I roll her nipple between my finger and thumb, and she moans aloud, slamming her lips closed tight in embarrassment.

"Don't be embarrassed, baby. I like that I make you feel good." I tug at her T-shirt until her braless breast is visible and then I suck it into my mouth. She can't control her rocking motion, and I lay still, letting her take what she needs. "I'm the only man who's gonna ever see you like this," I whisper, and she nods, closing her eyes and rocking faster.

"Ella!" We both freeze at the sound of Conner's voice. He'll put a bullet in my head if he sees us like this. Ella scrambles to get off me, and I stand quickly.

"Yes?" she shouts back.

"Come to my study. I need you to look at some of these figures for me. I can't make sense of them."

"Okay, I'll be a minute," she answers, straightening her hair and clothes. "You need to go," she whispers.

"I need some gym clothes. I'm meeting my friend for a workout and she forgot her kit at home."

"A female friend?" asks Ella suspiciously. I nod, pulling her towards me and kissing her hard. "I hate that."

"Baby, it's only you, you know this."

"There's loads of stuff in my wardrobe," she mutters, and then she leaves the room.

I walk into Ella's huge wardrobe and rummage around until I find some workout leggings and a short, cropped top. There are also multiple pairs of new trainers across one rack, and I take a couple pairs. Ten has small feet like Ella, so one of these will fit her.

Chapter Seven

LUCY

I spend the rest of the day anxious about Tag turning up again. I can't go out with him tonight. Noah would be so pissed. Keelan has spent the day annoying me, telling me how Tag is so much better than Noah. I hate that my friends hate him so much.

At exactly four o'clock, the door swings open and Tag enters holding two bags. "Let's go."

"Go where?" I ask, standing.

"For a workout," he says, throwing a bag towards me. It lands at my feet, and I pick it up gingerly, hoping he was joking about that part. "Quickly," he huffs.

I follow him from the shop. Keelan happily agreed to lock up for me if I went with Tag and didn't cause a fuss. "I don't work out," I confess.

"Well, there's a first for everything."

"How often do you work out?" I ask, almost running to catch up with his long strides.

"Every day, two or three times."

We reach the gym after a brisk ten-minute walk. I'm out of breath and my legs ache already. "Maybe I'd be better watching you. I'm no good at this sort of thing."

"If you continue to eat pastries every day, you'll spend your thirties paying for it," he says, pushing the glass door open. I stare open-mouthed before following him.

The receptionist smiles when she spots Tag. They high-five each other, and Tag signs us in. "Jo, this is a guest of mine," he says.

She grins at me. "Good luck. He'll work you hard." I groan, not liking the sound of that.

I go into the change room and peek inside the bag. There's a pair of workout leggings and a tight-fitted Lycra sports bra which I slip into. There're also two pairs of trainers, both new. I slip on the smaller pair and they fit perfectly. Suddenly, the door opens and Tag comes in. "Hey," I screech, "this is the girls' room."

He stands before me, looking me up and down. "You'll do," he says and then grabs my hand and leads me out of the changing room.

The gym is busy. It's filled with men almost as big and sexy as Tag, and I wonder if all women know about this cave of sexiness, because surely if they did, we'd all be queuing up for a peek. Tag smirks at me. "Close your mouth, Ten, you're drooling."

Tag leads me to the boxing ring in the centre of the gym. "We'll have a workout and then we can spar in here," he says, and I shake my head.

"Oh god, no, I can't do that."

"Of course, you can. I'll show you."

Jo wasn't exaggerating when she said Tag would work me hard. In the past, whenever I hit the gym—which wasn't often at all—I'd just had a quick run on the treadmill and maybe a go on the rower. But Tag, he makes me use every machine, and once I'm on a machine, he makes me stay on it, talking about reps and counting me down. My muscles are shaking in protest, and I feel slightly nauseous. He doesn't stand over me, which I first thought was a blessing. When he left me to get on with my sit-ups, I breathed a sigh of relief, but then he yelled at me from where he lifted weights. "Another twenty."

The guys around the gym smirk at my pleas for mercy. When he finally says, "Right, that's it, Ten," I could cry with happiness.

I glug down a bottle of water from the machine. Tag didn't head for the exit like I expected. Instead, he climbed into the boxing ring in the centre of the gym. My eyes bug out of my head. "Are you shitting me? I'm so exhausted, I could cry."

"Aw, come on, Ten, you're gonna pass up the opportunity to hit me?"

"I'm more worried about what will happen when you hit me."

Tag frowns and then shrugs. "I don't hit girls, Ten," he says, like that's obvious. It feels personal, like he's saying it because secretly he knows what happens between me and Noah. "Now, get in here."

I hold onto the bottom rope and pull myself up. There's nothing glamorous about the way I fall into the ring, and I wonder how the ring girls climb in with such grace and sexiness. "Well, that's harder than it looks," I mumble, brushing off my knees as I stand. Tag pushes my hands into some black boxing gloves and secures them with the Velcro straps. He picks up some thick pads and holds them in front of his body.

"Okay, show me what you've got," he says, changing his stance slightly.

"You just want me to hit the pad?" I ask warily, and he nods. "Are you sure? What if I miss and hit your face?"

"I can take it. I get hit all the time." I take a deep breath and then throw my hardest punch. It hits the pad, which is a bonus, but Tag doesn't move, not even an inch. "That was a good hit. Again."

"You didn't even budge. How do I hit hard enough to get someone out of my face?" I ask.

Tag eyes me for a second and then drops the pads to the floor. "It depends. If you're talking about being attacked and fighting back, you need to hit them hard enough to put them on their arse so you can run. Do anything to give yourself a head start. But in the ring, you need to work on your stance."

"Okay, well, show me how I do that."

Tag walks around and stops behind me. He places his hands on my hips and angles my body so that I'm almost side-on. I don't hear his words because my mind is too focused on the heat of his touch and how good it feels. He taps one of my legs just behind the knee and positions it so it's in front of my other leg. "You need to balance. If you get hit, you'll take the weight of the punch on this leg."

"I don't want to get hit. That's the whole point."

"In a ring, you're gonna get hit. It's kind of a given no matter how good you are. You have to learn to take the hits too."

"What about outside of the ring?" I ask. Tag moves back around until he's in front of me again and gives me a curious look.

"I don't understand, Ten."

"What if I'm out, say in a bar, and someone starts trouble with me, how do I protect myself?"

"You talk, use words. They're much more powerful than fists. I can show you how to throw a punch in the ring and how to protect yourself, but outside of that, you're better off with self-defence classes."

"Can you show me self-defence?"

"I guess so, but tell me the last time you needed to use self-defence while out in a bar," he asks with a laugh.

"You just never know." I don't want to tell him about Noah—it's my business.

"I think you should drink in some better bars. Besides, doesn't your man protect you? I know my woman wouldn't ever be put in a situation where she'd need to use self-defence."

"You can't always be around to protect her, just like Noah can't always be around to protect me."

"Nuh-uh," he says, shaking his head. "My woman won't be leaving my side, and when she does, she'll be with security. You can't ever leave a queen unprotected."

My heart swells. Maybe his words should worry me, because what woman wants a man who follows her around, but it makes me swoon, reminding me of the heroes I read about in romance books. "I think that's sweet," I whisper, and Tag rolls his eyes.

"I'm an old-fashioned kind of guy. Me Tarzan, she Jane, and all that bollocks. It's overbearing and I'm pretty sure it would drive her mad, but it's my way or no way."

"Who is she? Have you been together long?" I want to know all about him, even if that means asking questions I'm not going to like the answers to. Thinking about Tag with a woman on his arm kind of hurts my heart, which is ridiculous seeing as I've known the guy just a couple of hours.

"How long have you been with your guy?" he asks, avoiding my question.

"Too long. I met Noah in college around four years ago. Same kind of background and upbringing, so it made sense, yah know." I shrug, not knowing why I said it like we only got together for those reasons.

"What kind of background is that?" he asks, picking up the pads again.

"Rich, entitled, spoilt."

He cocks an eyebrow like this information surprises him. "You're just gonna admit all that shit?"

"I was talking more about his background." I shrug. "Mine too, I guess, but I hate it. I hate the money, the roles and responsibilities it brings, the expectations..." I trail off. I've never really said any of that out loud. Tyra and Bel know I hate the money and the assumptions it brings, but it's not something I really discuss.

"But you work hard and have a business. What's wrong with that?"

"My stepfather wanted to buy me the business, but I wouldn't let him. He paid outright behind my back, and I was so pissed." I shake my head at the memory. It was a rough time for me and my mum. Despite the fact they didn't agree with my career choice, they insisted on helping. Harold, my stepfather, hated the thought of me going to the bank for a loan, so he went behind my back and put an offer on the building where Frills, my business, is based. Of course, once I found out, I was outraged. He'd taken my decision from me, along with my choice. Tyra and Bel couldn't understand my anger. They thought I was being ungrateful, but I didn't want everyone to think I'd just walked into this business on Stepdaddy's hard-earned cash. I wanted to prove I could do it alone. Eventually, we agreed that I'd pay him back, just as if it was a bank loan, and since then, I've been a lot less angry about the whole thing. "What do you do, apart from fight?"

"Me?" He laughs and then shrugs his shoulders. "This and that. Like I said, we have a few family businesses."

"Why the cloak and dagger answer?" I ask. "What kind of businesses, all jewellers?"

TAG

I'm unsure of how much to tell Lucy. I want her to trust me enough for her to fall for me, and I can only do that if I open up enough to let her in, but not enough for her to ruin me when all of this ends. She's staring at me expectantly, waiting for my answer. I hold the pads up for her and nod. She gets into the stance I showed her and lightly taps the pads with her fists. It's cute really.

"We mainly buy and sell jewellery. Other than that, I work for a big organization. There's someone higher than me, and then me, I'm classed as the underboss. The organization generates a lot of money." Lucy gives me a quizzical look but continues to hit the pads.

"So, you have a lot of money too?"

"Does it matter?" I ask. I sense that it does, but not because she wants money. I think the idea of more money turns her off. She hates it, and I think she'd be much happier if I told her I had nothing and lived in the East End. "I have my own apartment. I work hard and I'm responsible for a lot of people. I make hard decisions, and like you, I don't flash my wealth around."

Lucy nods. "Sounds like you have a lot on your shoulders."

If only she knew. "Hence the need to burn off steam in the ring."

"Speaking of which, can we stop now? I'm exhausted."

I laugh. I really did work her hard, though not because she needs it because her figure is perfect. I just enjoyed watching her body work hard. "I'll take you for some food. I know a great place not far from here."

Half an hour later, I stop the car outside Kenny's restaurant. It's an American diner, we aren't dressed for somewhere more up-market, but for burgers, this is the best place for miles. Kenny isn't expecting me, but he owes me some money, so I thought I'd kill two birds with one stone. I hold the door open for Lucy to step inside, and Kenny spots me from the other side of the room. He pales slightly but hides it quickly and waves to me, forcing a large smile onto his fat face. "Boss, I haven't seen you for a while. It's great to see you."

"Kenny, good to see you. Table for two?"

He looks around the busy restaurant. "Erm, yeah, of course. Follow me."

"If you're busy, please don't worry," says Lucy politely.

"Oh, don't be silly. I'd never turn Tag away." He glances back at me before stopping at an empty table. "Please, take a seat and I'll get your drinks."

I slide into the red booth opposite Lucy, who looks very uncomfortable. "Two waters, please," I say, and he nods and then disappears to get them. Lucy watches him closely as he whispers into the ear of a passing waitress, who also eyes us before nodding and scuttling off to get our water.

"He didn't look too pleased to see you," states Lucy suspiciously.

"He didn't?" I shrug. "Maybe I should've booked ahead."

"He looks scared of you."

I watch Kenny glancing over at us nervously. "I don't know why. Some people get skittish around me because of my fighting career."

Lucy's mobile vibrates across the table and her boyfriend's name flashes on the screen. She stares at it for a moment and then smiles awkwardly. "Sorry, I have to get this." I nod, watching as she swipes across the screen and holds it to her ear. "Hey, baby," she coos. I can't be certain, but when she asked me earlier in the gym about self-defence, I immediately thought of this guy. She's got bruises that she's tried to cover with makeup. "I decided to go to the gym. How's work?" She nods. Why do people do that when they are on the phone? It's not like the other person can see them. "If it takes all night, then it can't be helped. Make sure you eat something, don't burn out."

I can see the disappointment on her face. This guy neglects his queen, and that gives me a perfect opportunity to swoop right in there. "Okay, I love you too. See you tomorrow." Once she's disconnected the call, she smiles. "Sorry about that."

"Not a problem. You didn't mention you were here with me."

"There's no need. I'm not doing anything wrong. Besides, he's very busy and stressed."

"Would he mind that you're eating dinner with another man?"

She thinks about my question. The waitress brings us our water, and I order us each a steak burger. I don't ask Lucy, but she doesn't seem to mind me ordering for her. "I don't think he'd mind. He doesn't really get jealous and doesn't mind me having male friends."

"I'm a ridiculously jealous person," I admit. "I'm slightly obsessive when it comes to my woman. Some might even say deranged." I add a little laugh to lighten the statement, but it's the truth. I'm completely obsessed with Ella, and once she's mine, I'll consume her life.

"Doesn't she mind?" asks Lucy.

"She doesn't know it yet. She isn't mine." I don't add anything further. That last sentence could mean anyone, including Lucy. She seems to think the same because she blushes. Our burgers arrive and Lucy's eyes light up. She takes a big bite and I smile. I like a woman who loves her food and isn't ashamed to eat in front of a man.

"Oh my god, this tastes so good," she says between mouthfuls. "If my mum could see me now, she'd have a fit."

"She doesn't agree with you eating burgers?"

"God, no. We don't eat food that requires us to use our hands, Lucy, darling," she says in a posh voice. "Whatever would they think of you at the country club? Poor Noah must despair."

I laugh, enjoying how she mocks the stuck-up rich people, even if they are her family. "You said you had a stepdad. What happened to your real dad?" I ask, tucking into my own burger.

"He left when I was a toddler. I don't remember him. Mum met Harold when I was ten. They dated for a while and then we moved in with him. Mum comes from money. Her parents are rich. She married for money, nothing else, but my real father wasn't from money. I think he was her little bit of rough." Lucy laughs and then it fades. "But I think she really loved him."

"Don't you ever think about finding him?" I ask.

Lucy shakes her head. "Not really. If he didn't want to stick around, then so what. I didn't need him. I guess, sometimes, I'd like to know more about him." She wipes her mouth on a napkin and throws it on her plate. She only managed half the burger, so I eat mine and then finish hers off. I hate waste.

Kenny approaches us. "Was everything okay, Tag?" he asks, and I nod. He knows I'm gonna ask him for my money. The fact I'm here in person is enough to scare him.

"Could we step into your office for a minute?" I ask, standing.

Kenny's eyes widen. "S-sure," he stutters.

I smile at Lucy, who is glancing back and forth between us. "I won't be long. Just a quick business thing."

I follow Kenny through the restaurant to the office at the back. I'm barely through the door before he's turning to face me and begging for more time. I sigh. I hate it when people beg. "Don't make this hard, Kenny," I groan. "I could have sent Tony. He wouldn't have been as nice as me, would he?" I ask, and Kenny shakes his head. Antonio is ruthless, which is why I hired him.

"I just need a few days, Tag, please. I've had problems with staff and the restaurant isn't doing as well as it was."

"Excuses, Kenny. It isn't my problem. You came to me for money, and did I make you wait for it?" I ask, referring to the ten-thousand-pound loan I gave him.

Kenny sighs. "No, boss."

"Then go get me the money from the till. I'm not asking for the full amount. I'm a reasonable guy, so five thousand will do for now."

Kenny's face pales further. "There isn't that much, Tag. I've barely made enough to pay my staff."

My jaw begins to tick, a sure sign I'm close to losing my shit. "So, what can you pay now?"

"A thousand?" He shrugs. My hand is around his throat and he's up against the wall in a split second. He coughs and splutters.

"I think you're taking me for a fool, Kenny," I growl. He can't respond, my grip is too tight. "And now, you've pissed me off. I'm trying to impress that girl, not scare the fuck out of her."

"S-S-Sorry . . ." gasps Kenny. His eyes dart to the door, from where I hear a sharp intake of breath. I glance back into the terrified eyes of Lucy. She turns and runs, slamming the office door closed.

"Fuck," I groan, releasing Kenny, who gasps and falls to his knees. "I'm sending Dan tomorrow at seven. Have my money by then."

I rush through the restaurant, bursting out into the fresh evening air. Lucy is halfway down the street, flailing her arms around to try and stop a black cab. One pulls in, and as she opens the door, I press my hand against it. "Stop," I order. I tap the roof of the cab, and he pulls away. "Let me explain." I haven't quite worked out what I'm going to say, but I know she can't leave like this. Lucy keeps her back to me, folding her arms across her chest. "Let's go back to my place. It isn't too far from here," I offer, but she doesn't respond. I sigh aloud.

"Lucy, you *will* hear me out, so you can walk back to my car and get in by yourself, or I can throw you over my shoulder and force the conversation." I wait for a second and then bend down and haul her up over my shoulder. She screams, hitting me on the back. "I told you to walk yourself. I don't like being ignored."

The street is busy, but no one so much as looks in our direction. This is London and odd things happen all the time. We look like a couple having a lovers' quarrel. I place her in my car and spot Antonio watching from his usual position, his motorbike always nearby wherever I am.

I lean into the vehicle and pull the seatbelt around her. She turns her head away from me, and I catch her scent, fruity and zesty, and I like it. I slam the door as Tony approaches, slowing his bike down by the driver's side. "Feisty," he remarks, smirking.

"Tell me about it. Can you do me a favour?" I hand him a piece of paper with Lucy's full name, date of birth, and address on it. "Pass this to Cruise. I need as much information as he can get on her, her mother, her absent father . . . I want as much as he can find." Tony tucks the paper into his leather jacket pocket.

"Right on it, boss. Do you need me anymore this evening?" I shake my head. I don't plan to leave my apartment for the rest of the evening. We fist-bump, and he speeds off.

I get into the vehicle and I'm met with frostiness. I have to make this right because I don't like the way it feels when she's mad at me.

We drive to my apartment in less than five minutes, and she remains silent the entire time. She doesn't get out of the car. Instead, she waits for me to open her door and take her by the hand. "Lucy, please stop judging me. Let me tell you why you saw what you saw."

"It's hard not to judge—the guy was terrified of you!" At least she's talking. I lead her into the apartment block, and she doesn't look in awe of the huge glass walls or the bright twinkly lights that bounce off the shiny floor like the other conquests do.

The security guy presses for the elevator, tipping his hat to me as we step inside. I insert my key card into the slot and the doors close. When the doors open again, we step directly into my penthouse apartment.

The huge living room is impressive. It's the main reason I bought the place. On one side of the room, the huge, custom-made couches curve into a long semi-circle. And on the opposite wall is a ridiculously large television that I hardly spend any time watching.

"Can I get you a drink?" I ask, shrugging out of my jacket. Lucy folds her arms across her chest and looks around the living room warily, shaking her head at my offer. I point to the couch, and she shuffles to the edge, perching like she doesn't plan on staying for long. "What you saw back there was a moment of craziness, a split second where I lost my temper. That doesn't usually happen," I lie. "Kenny cheated on my mum," I add, another lie, "and that's the first time I've seen him since then. He made a remark about her, and I lost my shit. I love my mum. She's my world."

Lucy eyes me sceptically. "Oh."

"I regretted it instantly. He really isn't worth my time, and I'm sorry you walked in on that."

"I don't like violence."

"Me either. I prefer to talk shit out, but then no man wants to hear his mother bad-mouthed."

"I guess," she mutters.

I take a seat next to her. "I had a great time tonight. I hope I haven't ruined it by that stupid mistake back there."

"I had a good time too . . ." She trails off, and I suspect she feels guilty because she has a boyfriend. We haven't done anything wrong yet, but I can tell she wants to. Her tongue keeps darting out and licking her lower lip. She wants me to kiss her.

Chapter Eight

LUCY

I'm not impressed by the big apartment or the flashy television that almost looks like a cinema screen. I wasn't impressed with the nice sporty car he drove or the fact that he had security men following him at a distance all evening. I certainly wasn't impressed when I saw him holding that poor restaurant owner by his throat, or the fact that he just lied to my face.

So, why in the hell do I want him to kiss me so bad? It's all I can think about—his lips on mine, his hands exploring my body in a way which I know Noah never will. I can tell, just by the look in Tag's eyes, that sex with him would be passionate, hungry, and exciting. With those thoughts comes a huge amount of guilt. I have a boyfriend, so I have no business being here and having these kinds of thoughts.

I stand abruptly and sigh. "I should go."

Tag's eyes bore deep into my own. I feel like he's reading my mind, and I blush. This guy is everything I should run from. He'll use me and spit me out, and I have too much at stake to risk that. Plus, he lied to me. I don't believe for one second that the guy cheated on his mum.

"Okay," he says, leaning back against the couch and kicking off his boots. I was expecting an argument. He picked me up and put me in his car to get me here, and now, he seems relaxed for me to just leave.

"Right, okay. Well, thanks for tonight."

I've taken a few steps when he shifts forward, leaning his elbows on his knees. "Of course, you could always stay for a while. It's not like he's back home waiting for you, is it?"

"That's not the point. I shouldn't be here."

"Why?" he asks. "We haven't done anything wrong," he pauses, "yet."

That's the word that scares me . . . yet. "What does that mean?"

Tag stands and moves towards me. "You know it'll happen. You feel it too. I must have thought about kissing your lips a thousand times tonight, and I don't know how much more control I've got, but I'd like to find out."

"It's not a good idea, I have a boy—" Tag presses his lips against mine, cutting off my words. I freeze, and Tag pulls back slightly. "Friend," I finish. He smirks and then his mouth is against mine again, his hands cupping my face as his tongue caresses mine in a slow, lazy kiss. I feel like I'm floating and the only thing keeping me on the ground is Tag's large hands.

He moves one hand into my hair and gently tugs a handful, angling my mouth the way that he wants it. His other hand trails to the front of my neck and rests there, not squeezing and not adding pressure, but having it there turns me the fuck on. I keep my hands hanging limply by my sides. I feel Tag's body shift closer until his front is pressed against mine, and there's no mistaking his erection is huge, pressing against my stomach.

When he releases me, I stumble backwards, putting some distance between us. "I lost my self-control," he whispers. "Forgive me."

"You can't do that again. I have a boyfriend, and I love him." Tag winces slightly but then nods once. "Sorry, it's just I've been with him a while now. We have a place together."

"But he hits you, he's never home, and I bet that right now, he's fucking his secretary or whoever works for smarmy lawyers these days."

I feel the tears rush to my eyes and I inwardly curse at the show of emotion. "Who said that? Who said he hits me?" I demand.

"The finger bruises on your upper arms, and the same type of bruises on your ankles. The fact you asked for techniques while we were sparring. And the yellow bruise under your eye that you think is covered by makeup. You don't love him, Lucy, but you're afraid to leave him."

"That's bullshit," I snap angrily. "You don't even know me. You've spent a few hours around me and now you suddenly know me inside out?" I laugh sarcastically. "Please. You're pissed because I've not dived into your bed and begged you to fuck me. I'm not one of those cheap whores you go around with."

"No?" he snaps. "Then why are you here? If you're so concerned about him, why are you here with me? Someone in love doesn't act that way, Lucy."

I slam my mouth shut. His words hurt, and I take a few steps towards the elevator. "Goodbye, Tag."

"Look, I'm sorry, I didn't mean that." He rushes towards me. "I don't want you to leave like this."

"This was a mistake," I say, pressing for the elevator and waiting patiently while it makes its way up. The doors open and I'm surprised to see a petite girl standing there. She has black mascara streaks down her cheeks, but apart from that, she's beautiful. Her long dark hair falls in waves down her back, and she looks trendy in a tight jeans and lace top that clings to her perfectly perky breasts. She pays no attention to me as she throws herself at Tag, who looks just as surprised as me.

"Ella," he whispers, catching her tiny frame in his arms. She wraps her legs around his waist and buries her face into his neck. Until that moment, I had no idea just how badly I wanted to do that same thing, and jealousy courses through me as I watch the pair wrapped together. He gently rubs her back. "What's wrong?"

"I can't take it anymore, Tag. I just needed to be in your arms. I'm sick of waiting."

Tag's eyes meet mine, and I shake my head. He avoided all talk of a girlfriend, and now, I feel like a fool. "Lucy, I'll get you a cab," he offers. The girl glances back over her shoulder like she's just realised I'm in the room.

"Who the fuck is Lucy?" she snaps.

"I'm a wedding planner." I smile. "Are you his lucky lady?" Her face changes and she looks back to Tag with a wide smile on her face.

"Baby, you're really serious about us?" she asks, failing to notice the late hour. Does she really believe that wedding planners work these kinds of hours? I wouldn't be surprised. Rich bitches think staff should work around them. I know because my mother is a rich bitch who thinks that way.

Tag gives an awkward smile, and she squeals before stuffing her tongue down his throat and grinding herself against him.

I step into the elevator. Tag opens his eyes, even though his girlfriend is still kissing him passionately, and gives me an apologetic stare. Whatever, I'm just glad I didn't do anything more with him. She could have walked in on us.

Once outside, I pull out my phone and call Tyra. I'm not ready to go home and sit alone. I need my girls. When she doesn't answer, I send her a text message asking where she is because I know she'll be in a nightclub somewhere. While I wait for her reply, I flag down a black cab. "Where to, love?" he asks.

"Head for Cargo," I say, reading the text from Tyra.

TAG

I disentangle myself from Ella. She's never turned up here before, and that was a close call. "How did you get here? Where's your security?"

Ella rolls her eyes and she suddenly reminds me of a stroppy teenager. "Don't you start. You sound just like my father."

"For a good reason, El. You know you can't just leave the house on your own." I pull out my mobile. If I don't tell Anton or Conner that she's here and they find out, they'll get suspicious.

"What are you doing?" she snaps, snatching my phone from my hand.

"I'm calling your brother. He'll be going nuts not knowing where you are. How did you even get out of that place without being spotted?" Their house is more secure than a prison. "And why the hell did you come here? Your father will stick a bullet in me."

"Don't be so dramatic. I wanted to see you, and I'm so sick of sneaking around. I'm supposed to be sleeping at Katie's house," she says. That makes more sense. "I gave security the slip and got out the back, and Katie won't tell. Nobody knows I'm here."

"Ella, that isn't the point. We need to be careful." We've never been alone like this before, and I'm not sure how much control I have now that no one can interrupt us. She runs her hand along my chest and peeks up at me with those baby blue eyes.

"You finally have me alone and you're worried about my brother and father? We have a few hours together, let's make the most of it." She doesn't mean sex. She means other stuff, like kissing, touching—stuff I did when I was a teenager. Not that I mind. I love her, and I respect her decision to wait, but with no one around, it's going to be hard to control myself.

She stands on her tiptoes and kisses me gently on the mouth. Taking the kiss deeper, her hands run through my already messy hair. I close my eyes and see Lucy, her bright blue eyes piercing me. My eyes shoot open in surprise. Lucy is the last person I should be thinking about, even if her kiss was amazing. I remind myself that Lucy is part of the game, collateral damage for the thing I want more than anything. When Ella pulls away, I'm hard. She smirks and rubs her hand over the bulge in my pants. "Who was the girl?"

"I told you, she plans weddings," I say, tucking her soft hair away from her eyes.

"I'm not stupid, Tag. Who the fuck was she?"

I sigh. Ella plays a good version of dumb, but she's exactly like her father and you can't get fuck all past her. "She's part of my plan to get you."

"Explain."

"She came to an after-fight party. She was cold as ice, a real bitch. The deal is, I get her to fall for me, and in return, your brother supports me when I talk to your father about us."

Ella steps back from me. "And if you lose?"

"Your brother gets my apartment."

"But you love this place," says Ella, looking around.

"I know, but I love you more. Once it's official that I'm head of my family, I'll be a step closer to earning your father's respect. With Anton on our side, he'll be more likely to let it happen."

"How do you plan to make this ice queen fall for you?"

"I don't know. I haven't figured that part out yet. I'm just gonna be my charming self."

Ella laughs. "Start with flowers, maybe a meal somewhere uptown."

"No, she's not like that. Money won't impress her." Ella screws up her face like she doesn't understand the concept of someone not being impressed by expensive things. "She's from money, so it doesn't impress her. I thought it would be easy and then I found that out. Plus, she's got a boyfriend."

"So," Ella shrugs, "she can still fall for you while she has a boyfriend. Sneaky is your middle name. Invite them to your fight."

"She won't come. He's a lawyer, always busy."

"Then send VIP tickets to his office. If he's rich, he'll be used to being invited to events. You need to excite her, and what better way to do that than invite them there and flirt with her under his nose?"

I think it over. It sounds like a plan, and after tonight's fuck-up, she won't willingly come. Inviting her boyfriend is a great plan, and I could blame it on marketing sending tickets out if she bothers to question it.

"That could work. I've asked Cruise to find out more about her. Hopefully, he'll come up with this guy's firm." My phone buzzes. Ella still has a hold of it, so she glances down and rolls her eyes, holding it out for me. I take it and accept the call. "Conner," I say in greeting. Ella rubs her hand over my crotch, and I scowl at her, trying to move away. She follows, smirking, and then jumps onto my back and kisses along my neck. "Yes, boss, she's just turned up here. I was about to call Anton."

Ella climbs around my body until she's clinging to my front like a baby monkey. I wrap one arm around her, and she snuggles into my neck. "Yeah, I'll drive her back now." She pouts at me, but if I'm honest, I'm pleased that I won't have to worry about my self-control now.

I drive her home in silence. She hates this part of her life, as she'd prefer to be free. "You need to stop sulking like a child." I sigh, stopping at a red traffic light.

"Shut up, Tag. You don't know what it's like."

"Don't tell me to shut up," I snap. "We're trying to keep you safe."

"I don't need you to. I can look after myself."

"Grow up, El. Walking around London alone puts you in danger. You know how many people would like to get at us?"

She sighs. "I can't wait to leave home and marry you. I need to be free." The light changes to green and I pull off.

"You think all this will stop when we get married?" I laugh and glance at her. "Baby, you won't be going anywhere without me or security."

"So, I'm leaving one prison for another?" She huffs, "Fuck that."

"Watch your mouth," I hiss. "What the fuck's gotten into you? And what does that even mean, fuck that?"

"I might be your wife, but I'll be an independent woman. I'll be doing what I want."

"Yeah, with me or security watching over you."

"What if I want to meet my friends for a drink?"

"Jesus, Ella, you sound like a miserable, nagging wife already. Let's just take one day at a time. Your father might not allow it anyway."

"Will you have sex with that woman?" she asks. I wasn't expecting the question and I falter, not answering straight away.

"No, of course not," I lie.

"Bullshit." It's not like Ella thinks I'm saving myself for our wedding night. She knows I have sex with other women. We aren't officially together, and we've never really set up any rules. I just knew that I was gonna marry her one day and I made that clear to her. Other than that, we've just been living separate lives apart from the odd sneaky kiss and fondle.

"What do you want me to say, Ella? You're acting weird all of a sudden, turning up at my apartment, asking questions. I'm not used to it."

"Well, get used to it if we're getting married because once that's done, you won't be having sex with other women." We reach her house, and I press the key fob to open the security gates.

I stop the car, and she practically dives from the vehicle and takes the front steps two at a time to get away from me. My head is spinning as I follow at a slower pace, trying to work out what tonight was all about.

When I get inside, Conner is standing at the bottom of the stairs yelling up at Ella. She's almost at the top step before he commands her to come back down to him. As she reaches the bottom, he backhands her, and she falls into the wall, clutching her cheek. "You sneak out, you ignore your phone, you walk back into my house with the attitude of an ungrateful little cunt, and then you walk away when I'm talking to you?" My hands curl into fists, but I can't step in because it'll cost me my life, though every cell in my body is screaming at me to help her. "Where did you go?"

"Just to see Tag. I was bored and wanted some air." Conner hits her again, and this time, she cries out, tears rolling down her cheeks. "You're a liar."

"I'm not lying," she protests. "I'm not."

"Why would you go to see Tag?" He turns to me for an explanation, and I open my mouth to tell him the truth, fuck the consequences, but Ella stands again, gripping the wall for support.

"It's not his fault. I went to meet a man, but he didn't turn up and Tag's place was nearby, so I went there for a lift back to Nat's."

"A man?" repeats Conner, his attention back on his daughter. She begins to cry harder, and I glare at her. Why would she get herself into more trouble? "How have you met a man?"

"On Tinder," she mutters, and I wonder if Conner's head will explode when he growls aloud and makes a move towards her.

"Conner," comes Alison's voice. His wife enters with such grace that we all turn to her. "Stop."

"Get her out of my sight, Tag, before I fucking kill her," orders Conner, walking towards his wife.

I take Ella by the arm and pull her up the stairs towards her room. Once inside, I slam the door. "Why the fuck did you say that?" I hiss.

"Because if you tell him about us, he'll ruin it, and I can't handle that."

"But now he thinks you're a whore," I snap.

"Good, let him think that for a while. Plus, it might help when you offer to take me on."

I sigh, swiping a thumb over her wet cheek, then place a gentle kiss on her forehead. "I hate it when he acts like that."

"Then hurry up and get me away from here," she says with a sad smile.

Chapter Nine

♥

LUCY

I roll onto my back to find Noah looking down at me. He smiles as I stretch out, checking the clock for the time. It's ten in the morning and my head is pounding. Meeting the girls wasn't the best idea now that I have a hangover from hell. "You stink like a bar," says Noah, screwing his face up.

"You worked all night?" I ask, and he shakes his head.

"Nah, I got home around five this morning, but you were so out of it, I left you to sleep."

"Yeah, I met with the girls. Bad idea," I mutter, and he laughs.

"Well, to make up for last night, I got us tickets to go somewhere tonight."

"Aw, you didn't have to do that," I smile, "but I'm excited to spend time with you. Where are we going?"

Noah kisses me on the cheek. "It's a surprise. I have to go and run some errands. There's money on the side, so go get a new outfit, something sexy. We'll be leaving here at six."

I wait until he's gone before I take a shower. I have a million outfits and really don't want another, so I decide to go into work for a few hours and catch up on emails.

Almost an hour later, I'm at my desk sketching a centrepiece idea when the shop door opens. Penelope breezes in, her arms full of shopping bags. She dumps them near my desk and flops down on a nearby chair. "Oh my god, I never thought I'd hate shopping, but today, I've seriously had enough."

I peek into one of the bags and spot a black lace bra. "Are you treating Wyatt?"

"No, I am not," she huffs. "I'm treating myself. Francesca is meeting us here. She's bringing lunch."

"Fran is up before mid-day on a Saturday, wow," I joke. Francesca is the single one in our group and she's always out partying. She works in promotion and her work often takes her to some great nightclubs.

"Anyway, going back to Wyatt, we aren't talking."

"That's not like you two." Penelope and Wyatt never really argue. Penelope is very chilled and tries to avoid confrontation. Not because she's shy and quiet, but because if you piss her off, she turns into a psycho.

"I've hardly seen him this week. He doesn't give any real excuse and says I'm nagging." She scoffs. "Me, nag!"

"That doesn't sound like you," I agree with a grin. "Is he stressed?"

"Stressed? The man doesn't know the meaning of the word stressed." The door opens again and Fran enters holding a large brown paper bag.

"Ladies." She smiles as I stand, and we kiss cheeks. I haven't seen Fran for a few weeks and note how well she looks. The smells from the paper bag fill the office and my stomach grumbles. "What are we talking about?" she asks, opening the bag and setting out sandwiches.

"Penelope was just saying how she hasn't seen Wyatt this week. He accused her of being a nag." Fran raises her eyebrow, and we smirk at each other. "I just asked if he's stressed, but she doesn't seem to think it's that."

"He has a lot of responsibility, Penelope. Don't be so harsh," says Fran.

"What do you know of his responsibilities?" Penelope huffs. "You can't comment when you don't have a boyfriend."

"Penelope," I admonish.

"What?" she shrieks. "It's true."

"You're being a bitch," I mutter, opening a grilled cheese sandwich. Penelope's older than the rest of us by only a few months, but she's always taken on the role of big sister. She'll often say whatever she's thinking and expect us to be okay with it.

"I think he's having an affair," Penelope blurts out. I stop mid-chew and lock eyes with Fran, both of us too shocked to speak. I swallow what's in my mouth.

"Penelope, I'm sure it's nothing like that," I reassure her.

"Oh, please, he hasn't come near me. He talks to me like shit, and he's never home."

I sigh. "Neither is Noah, but I don't think he's having an affair."

"He probably is, with that whore who's fucking his father," she snaps, and I gasp. She winces and then sighs. "Sorry, I didn't mean that. I'm just upset."

"Well, that's no reason to be such a cow," snaps Fran, rubbing my arm in sympathy. "And to be honest, if you behave like this towards Wyatt, then I'm not surprised he's going elsewhere."

Penelope stands, grabbing her shopping haul. "I don't know why I put up with you all," she yells and then stomps out. Fran shrugs her shoulders and offers a small smile.

"Ignore her. Noah wouldn't cheat on you."

"Do you think Wyatt would cheat on Penelope?" I ask, and she shrugs again.

Later in the evening, I get ready for our surprise night out. I decided on a long, clingy black dress with long slits up each side. But when I finally emerge from the bedroom, Noah doesn't give me a second glance. I feel annoyed since I tried to make a special effort for him, as it's been a while since he's taken me out like this, just the two of us. I've spent hours curling my hair and painting my nails, so his lack of attention only deepens the thought that he's having an affair, thanks to Penelope planting that little seed.

Our driver slows the car outside a rundown building. I glance over to Noah, who's staring down at his phone. "Noah," he looks up and smiles, "where are we?"

"You'll see. I don't think we've ever had a date like this." The driver opens my door, and I step out into the cool evening air. A few other people are approaching the building, so I know this date will not be just the two of us like I was expecting. Noah takes my hand and leads the way.

A man in a suit steps forward as we enter, and Noah hands him two tickets. The man checks a list and then hands us the tickets back and smiles. "Good evening, Mr. Fielding. Seats are reserved at ringside. Your number is on the ticket."

Noah looks at the ticket. "Number ten?" he asks, and the man nods, opening another door for us to step inside. My heart beats hard in my chest. *Ringside. Number ten.* I think I'm going to throw up as Noah leads us through the busy room.

"What are we doing here?" I finally ask as we stop by a table with a large number ten in the centre. I know it can't be coincidence, so I glance around, trying to see if I can spot Tag.

"It's a charity boxing match," explains Noah, shrugging out of his jacket and draping it over my shoulders. "You're shivering," he adds. I don't tell him that I'm not cold, that I'm shivering from nerves and anxiety. "It was a special invitation, hand delivered late last night."

"Didn't your father want the tickets?" I ask, taking my seat.

"No, it's not his thing." Noah waves at someone across the room. "Do you mind if I pop over and say hello to someone I know through work?" he asks. I shake my head, needing some time to gather myself.

I watch as he shakes hands with another suited man and then I look around the room, trying to find the way to Tag's dressing room. I see people going back and forth through a door at the far side of the room and decide to try there. I need to find out what he's playing at and if he plans to tell Noah about our little kiss. The thought makes me feel sick. When I reach the door, a man stops me, putting his arm out in front of me. "Nobody is allowed back here," he growls. I look down at his meaty hand and then directly into his eyes.

"Tell Tag that number ten is here to see him. He'll want to see me."

He eyes me for a second and then speaks into his mouthpiece. We wait for a second before he drops his arm and nods. "Straight through there," he instructs, pointing to another door.

I step into the room and it's chaos. There are important-looking men everywhere, and in the centre of the room is Tag. He's sitting on a stool while a man tapes his hands. I recognise another man to his left from the last afterparty. He's talking into Tag's ear as Tag listens and nods. The girl who turned up at Tag's apartment is standing next to a large, suited man with a stern-looking face who gives off vibes that he's a big deal around here. Ella watches me but doesn't acknowledge me with a smile or even a frown.

Tag finally looks up and spots me. He doesn't smile either, and I wonder if I've jumped to conclusions. I'm debating whether to back out of the room. I don't feel like confronting him now that all these people are in here, but before I can retreat, Tag is walking towards me. "Ten," he says, his voice gruff. "What are you doing here?"

"Erm," I glance around, hoping to be rescued from this awkward situation, "Noah got tickets."

"The promotional team send them out to offices around the area. Nothing to do with me, Ten. Could you stick around after the fight so we can talk?"

I suddenly feel stupid. Of course, he didn't invite us, that would be weird. "Maybe. I'm with Noah, though, so it could be weird."

Tag looks around, and the man next to Ella is staring at us with interest. Tag takes me by the arm and marches me from the room. I try to shrug him off, but he has a firm hold. He takes me farther down the corridor and pushes me into another room full of cleaning products. I screw my nose up, "Why in here?"

"I just wanted to apologise for last night."

"No need. It was fun, but we both have someone else, so it shouldn't have happened."

"About that . . . Ella isn't with me. She's Anton's little sister, and we're close, but it's nothing like that. Her father and brother are overprotective and they won't allow it."

"But she talked about weddings and she seemed really into you," I begin.

"She wants that to happen, but I've got to let her down gently, so she doesn't tell her father I've hurt her. He'll kill me, and I'm not exaggerating."

"So, let me get this straight. You've messed around with your best friend's sister and now you've got to get out of it without upsetting her?" I laugh.

He sighs. "Basically, yeah."

"Wow, what a mess."

"Look, I have to go. I'm out in ten and I still have to warm up. I'm glad you're here, and I'll try and catch up after the fight." He leaves the closet, and I stare at the closed door. He seemed distant, nothing like last night.

Noah is back at our table, and when I see the number ten, I kick myself for not asking Tag about it. That can't be coincidence.

"Where did you go?" asks Noah. "I got you wine because I didn't know what you wanted," he adds, placing a large glass of white wine in front of me. I don't want to point out that I hardly ever drink wine unless it's free with a meal.

"I needed the bathroom," I lie.

TAG

I wasn't prepared for Lucy to just turn up in my room like that. I thought she'd give me daggers from the side of the ring, but her having the balls to walk into a room full of my team like that, well, it impressed me. The bell rings to announce the first round and I shake my head, trying to clear thoughts of Lucy from my mind and concentrate on winning this fight. It's just for charity, so I don't have to drag it out because there are ten other fights tonight.

Rolling my eyes, I watch my opponent bouncing around the ring, jabbing thin air and making hissing noises. I catch him by surprise, knocking his chin with a right hook and then landing a left to his eye. His head snaps back, and when he rights himself, I go in again, not giving him a chance to hit me once. Conner is seated ringside, and I can hear him yelling at me to take my opponent down. He's brutal and likes me to show no mercy. The bell rings again and we both head to our corners. As a water bottle is squirted into my mouth, Conner shouts at me from where he stands on the floor. "Stop playing around with him," he shouts. "It shouldn't have even lasted a round."

I ignore him as my trainer smooths Vaseline over my brows. I don't like cuts and this helps the opponent's gloves to slide off my face. "Better take him in this round, Tag. Conner's going nuts." I nod. I can see Lucy over the other side of the ring. Her boyfriend is on his phone, paying her no attention, and it pisses me off. She deserves his attention. When I look over my shoulder at Ella, she's chatting to her mother while filing her nails.

The bell sounds again and the ring clears. I stand, cracking my neck from side to side. When my opponent steps into my space, I lay into him. Each blow gives me a sick satisfaction. My opponent falls to his knees and then crashes onto his front, laying like a starfish. The referee counts him out, then grabs my hand and holds it in the air, indicating that I'm the winner. That feeling of pride never gets old.

The ring fills with both our teams. I'm patted on the back and congratulated, though I don't know why. This was a small fight, nothing compared to what I'm used to. Ella presses a kiss to my cheek and whispers her congratulations into my ear. It sends a shiver down my spine, and I'm reminded of how much I love her. Anton joins me, slapping me hard on the back. "Numbers haven't gone out tonight, my friend. There are far too many rich bitches here for you."

"I thought we'd put a hold on that, Anton. Remember our deal?" I wipe my brow on the towel that my trainer hands me.

"You want to stop all the games for one girl?" he asks doubtfully.

"Yeah, this is a bigger deal than normal."

"She must be hard work if you want to put all your energy into her." He smirks. "I suddenly feel very confident that I'm gonna win this. I might pop round to measure up the apartment next week."

I spot Lucy walking towards the bar and I dash from the ring, ignoring Anton's over-confidence. This is my chance to lay my feelings on thicker. Her boyfriend is still engrossed in his phone as I pass him. I stand behind Lucy, pressing close to her back, then I lean into her ear. "After a fight," I whisper, "I'm always horny."

Lucy laughs. "And you're telling me that because . . ."

"Because in this room full of rich, beautiful women, I only see you." I take her hand and lead her away from the bar. We slip in and out of people and take the back entrance out onto a side street, hidden in a dark alleyway. I turn to her and push her against the wall, and without a word, I kiss her. I make sure that my body is angled in just the right way to keep her still so she can't escape. I thrust my tongue into her mouth and wrap my hands into her hair. Eventually, she comes to her senses and pulls away, panting.

She gasps. "We can't do this."

"Why?"

"I have a boyfriend," she cries in frustration.

"You mean that guy you've sat beside all evening while he ignores you?"

"Don't judge my relationship. You know nothing about us."

"I know he doesn't excite you," I risk, moving back to her and backing her up to the wall again. "I know you want to be pinned against this wall, and you want me to fuck you."

Lucy sucks in a wistful breath. "Stop."

"You want me to bury my head between your legs and taste you."

I see a hint of a blush on her moonlit face. "Tag, please."

"I bet if I was to touch you here," I press my hand to the gap between her legs, "I'd find you soaking wet." I slide my hands to cup her arse, pulling her against my throbbing cock. "I know you feel the pull, just like I do."

"Tag, you're overstepping."

"You want me to." Who the fuck is she kidding? It's obvious she wants me to, or she wouldn't keep letting me drag her off into dark corners.

"Tag, are you out here?" It's Ella's voice that echoes out into the silence. We both freeze, and then Ella appears at the entrance to the alleyway. We're hidden from view behind the large industrial bins. "Tag," she shouts again, and I smirk at Lucy, who looks terrified.

"Laters, Ten," I whisper, and then I push myself away from the wall and head towards Ella.

"What are you doing out here? Everyone's asking where you went," she says.

"I needed some air," I say. Once I'm closer to Ella and out of Lucy's earshot, I take her upper arm and pull her away from the alley. "What the hell are you doing, El? I told you what I have to do so we can be together, and then you keep turning up like this."

"Sorry," she whispers, glancing behind us. "Anyway, she'll like the danger. It makes everything more exciting."

"Make what exciting? Every time I get a second alone with her, some fucker interrupts us."

"You almost look disappointed by that, Tag," mutters Ella, and I don't miss the annoyance that passes over her expression.

"You know why I'm doing this. Your brother only understands games and deals."

"Have you told her all about me?" she asks.

I frown, shaking my head. What does she expect me to say? "No. If I tell her, then she'll see how much I care for you. Women are good at that. I've maybe mentioned that you have a little crush on me."

Ella gasps, horrified. "Oh great, so now, I look like some desperate little stalker."

I drop my hand from the small of Ella's back as Conner approaches. We shake hands, and he pats my shoulder. "You left after the fight. We have things to discuss," he says, then he glances at Ella. "The driver is waiting out front for you and your mother, Ella."

"I was hoping to stay for the celebrations," she mutters, and he shakes his head. She knows better than to argue with him, so she goes off to find her mother. I follow Conner into another room and find Anton is inside waiting for us.

"I spoke with the other families. As you know, we're all in agreement that you should step up as head of the Corallos. The other families want to see how serious you are about taking over from him, and to keep your family in the organisation, they have reiterated what we discussed before."

"Right," I say, straightening my spine. I hadn't had a chance to talk with Anton about it. Our little bet seems to have taken over.

"Your father has become an embarrassment to us all. He has shamed the families and made a mockery of our beliefs and laws. We don't care about the money, but we won't let what he's done slide. Therefore, for your family to remain part of our organisation, you'll need to put a hit out on him as soon as possible. Within the next few days."

My world spins, my heart hammers inside my chest, and I'm paranoid that Conner will hear it. "You said I had until the end of the month, and now, you're saying you want me to put a hit on him immediately, as in right now?"

"Yes. It will show outsiders that we don't tolerate fools, not even our own, and it will prove to the families that you're still loyal to us. They have their reservations about how much you knew."

"But *you* know I'm loyal to you, Conner. My father was an addict who lost control. I'm nothing like him."

"Still, you're his blood, and we need solid proof that your loyalty is with us and not him. The families are tired of this being dragged out. They want to see actions."

I watch as Conner leaves, then stare at the closed door for a few minutes before turning to Anton. "Shit, how the hell am I gonna get out of this?"

"You're not. It needs to be done, Tag. We tried to help him, but he'll be expecting this. He's had time to make peace with it."

"He's my father, Anton. No matter what he did, it was for a reason. He loved the families and he'd do anything for them. What he did must have been out of desperation."

"Tag, you don't need to tell me. I get it, it's why I helped you get him out of here, but you know that without the organisation, you and your mother are dead. So, get it done and carry on. If you want to be head of your family, it comes with responsibilities."

I knew this, but I assumed Conner would put the hit out, not me. After all, he's the head of the whole organisation. "And you know he'll send a shitload of tests your way, starting with this." Anton holds out a piece of paper, which I take from him. "This guy needs taught a lesson. He spoke out against you."

"Who is he? I've never heard of him before." The name scrawled in black ink is Aiden Tollero.

"No one important, a soldier, and not a very good one."

Being at the top of the family—under Conner, of course—we don't really have much to do with the soldiers. They do all the families' running around and the dirty work. There are lots of them, and they come with their own hierarchy, so this guy must be very low in the ranks if I've not heard his name before. "What did he say?"

"He bad mouthed your ability to step up as underboss. Michael caught wind of it and passed it my way. We don't need soldiers forgetting how to behave. Plus, I think that maybe this is a test from my father. Michael will be keeping a close eye to see if this guy faces repercussions." Michael is Conner's adviser and right-hand man.

"Well, let's go find the piece of shit then. It's been a while since I got to do this."

Chapter Ten

TAG

I'm sitting in the front passenger seat watching the warehouse. Tony is in the driver's seat, and Anton is in the back. "Are you sure that's him?" I ask, and Tony nods once. "Then what are we waiting for?"

The guy we're looking for went inside minutes ago, and there doesn't seem to be anyone else around. We all step from the vehicle and make our way towards the warehouse. It's in a shitty part of London, not somewhere I'd usually come.

Aiden Tollero is sitting in a reclining deck chair with a set of headphones on and his eyes closed. There's a girl laying on the hard floor, naked. She watches us enter the warehouse but makes no move to tell Aiden, who is happily nodding in time to the beat that pumps through his headset. "You need to get out of here, bitch," says Tony, and she sits herself up slowly.

"She's seen us now, just put a bullet in her," mutters Anton.

I stand over Aiden, and he opens one eye. Once he spots me, he opens them both wide in surprise. I pull the headset from his ears and smirk down at him. "Evening, Aiden."

"Mr. Corallo," he squeaks, pulling himself to sit.

"Who's your friend?" asks Anton, and Aiden glances at the girl who looks so strung out, her features are devoid of any emotion.

"She's sampling the stuff for us," blusters Aiden, his cheeks flushed in fear as his eyes dart around the warehouse.

"Liar," I say firmly. "Who is she?"

"I swear, man, she's no one important, just a whore trying the new shit we're pushing."

I march over to where the girl is sitting on the floor and grip a handful of her hair. "So, if I do this, you won't give a shit?" I growl, tugging down my zipper and reaching inside for my cock.

"No, boss, wait," stutters Aiden, diving from his chair in a panic. I knew she meant something to him, it's all over his face, the pussy. I shove the girl away from me, and she lands in a heap, her face dazed and pale. I pull out my .22 and press it to the girl's head. "Please..." Aiden begins to beg, but I pull the trigger, blowing the girl's brains across the concrete floor. Aiden yells out, but it's too late.

"You think I'm not good enough, Aiden? You think you can bad mouth me and say I don't have it in me to be the underboss?" His stare is fixed on his now dead girlfriend. "You sell my drugs, you make me money, and we don't have a problem. You bad mouth me again, and I'll kill everyone close to you. Kids, wife, sister, mother... I don't have a preference." I step over the girl's body and head for the exit. "Now, get this mess cleaned up and get back to work."

LUCY

I stare down at Noah's flaccid cock. I've tried everything, including the sexy lingerie I have on right now, just to entice him into a bit of kinky action. He doesn't look one bit embarrassed by the fact he isn't remotely turned on by me. "Maybe we can watch some porn?"

I suggest, because after my brief run-in with Tag earlier tonight, I'm horny as fuck.

"Actually, I'm not feeling it tonight, babe," says Noah, gripping me by the hips and removing me from his lap.

"Are you joking?" I snap. "Noah, we haven't done it all week. I need something," I huff. "Anything would be good."

"Well, I'm not in the mood." Noah stands and pulls his boxer briefs back on. "And I don't like this whole," he points his finger in my direction, screwing his face up in disgust, "whore look you have going on."

I look down at my little black lacy number. "I got these from Victoria's Secret in the hope it'd spice us up a little," I snap, standing to meet him head on so he can't walk out of the room on me. "I spent a fortune to look this good."

"Well, clearly, it was a waste of money because it's done nothing for me."

"Maybe it's me who does nothing for you," I hiss. "Maybe it's someone else who's got your attention."

"What the hell are you talking about?"

"I'm talking about your new little office whore, Emma."

"Don't be ridiculous, Lucy... and put some damn clothes on." He throws his white shirt at me, and I catch it as it hits my face. "Get out of my way."

"No, where are you going?"

"I need to escape you and your crazy accusations." He sighs, trying to step around me.

"No," I hiss, "I'm sick of you walking out on me."

"I mean it, Lucy, move." The vein in his forehead begins to tick.

"Why are we even together if you can't bear to be in the same room as me, Noah?" I demand, "Things get tough and you just walk out.

Where do you go this late at night? Where are you when you're gone until the early hours?"

Noah isn't used to me questioning him, but I've had enough of him and his disappearing acts. The lack of attention is killing me. He tries to pass me again, but I block his path a second time. I know that I'm on dangerous ground, but right now, I just need answers.

"You're not leaving, Noah. Not until we've sorted this once and for all. Do you even love me at all?" His hand lashes out, striking me across the face, and then he grips me by the hair and pushes my face into the mattress of the bed.

"Stop trying to antagonise me, you stupid bitch. I don't want to fuck you when you look like a cheap tart. Get some damn clothes on. Maybe I'll be turned on when you find your self-respect."

"Did you know Emma is fucking your father?" It's a low blow, but I need to know if he has feelings for Emma. Noah uses my hair to drag me onto my back, then he climbs over me, placing a knee either side of my waist. His expression is dark and full of rage. It's the answer I needed. His hands wrap around my neck and he squeezes until I'm gasping for breath.

"How dare you use my father in your sick games?" he growls, slapping me across the face while keeping one hand on my neck. I start to panic, wheezing while trying to pry his fingers from their grip. "I can't even be around you right now." He releases his hold, and I cough violently as I draw air into my lungs. My head spins with dizziness, and I watch as Noah leaves the room, slamming the door hard behind him. Seconds later, I hear the front door.

I lay there for at least another ten minutes trying to figure out why we're still together when neither of us seems very happy. A knock on the door brings me from my thoughts. Noah sometimes storms out only to come back minutes later with a half-arsed apology.

I unlatch the door and leave him to open it. I'm not going to make this easy for him. For once, we're going to sit down and have an honest conversation, one where I lay my cards on the table.

I'm half conscious of the fact that I'm still wearing the black lace bodice with matching garters and stockings. It might piss him off more that I haven't changed or covered up.

"Ten, are you trying to kill me?" I spin around at the sound of Tag's voice.

"What the hell . . ." The intense stare as Tag runs his eyes over my body thrills me. It was the reaction I'd wanted from Noah. His chest heaves and his hands hang by his sides, neither of us making a move.

"I watched him leave but knowing he left you looking like this makes me wonder what the fuck is wrong with him."

The first words that come into my head are, "We argued," followed by, "it's from Victoria's Secret." I feel my face turning crimson. Why does his presence take away my ability to form a proper sentence?

"Tell me to leave," he growls, taking a step towards me.

"Why?" I ask, my heart pounding hard in my chest.

"Because you have a boyfriend," he says, taking another step closer. We're only two steps from each other now, and he's staring at my lips.

"He said I looked like a cheap tart," I say quietly.

"If you don't tell me to leave, I'm going to do all kinds of bad things to you, Lucy. Things I've been wanting to do to you since the day I met you." He takes another step forward, and I feel the heat from his body.

"What if Noah comes home?"

"Then he can watch." He closes the distance, sweeping me up into his arms. I wrap my legs around his waist and my back hits the wall as his mouth clashes against mine in a hungry, desperate kiss. "I'm gonna fuck you hard and fast, then I'll do it again slowly." He pulls the lace down to uncover my breasts, staring for a moment before taking a nipple into his mouth.

Then, I feel him fumble around with the button on his jeans, releasing himself. "Ten, I'm gonna need to know what these marks and bruises are from?" he pants, nodding at the red marks along my chest and neck. He gets a condom from his back pocket before shoving his jeans down to his ankles.

"Noah gets pissed off easily," I whisper. It's the first time I've told anyone other than Penelope.

"You're gonna tell me everything," he says with a firm tone. "But first, I've gotta take care of you." He rips the condom open and sheaths himself. He places my hands on his broad shoulders, lining himself at my entrance. "I don't know if I can be gentle right now," he mutters, pressing his forehead against my shoulder.

That's good because I don't want him to be gentle. "Don't hold back, Tag . . . fuck me."

He groans. "You have no idea what those words are doing to me," he murmurs. He pushes against my entrance, and I'm immediately aware of his size as he slowly enters into me. I squeeze his shoulders, gasping each time he moves another inch. He stills, giving me a minute to adjust. "You okay?" he asks, and I nod. He groans as he fills me, squeezing my thighs. "Fuck, Ten, you feel too good."

I'm impatient, needing to feel the urgent passion we just had. "If I feel so good, why are you taking your time?"

He smirks. "You sure you're ready?" I nod, and he adjusts position, placing one hand above my head, leaving the other under my thigh. He withdraws slow, watching my face carefully, and then he slams back into me hard, groaning in pleasure. He pulls out of me, lowering me to the floor, and I catch a glimpse of his erection. Fuck, he's huge. No wonder I felt so full.

He smirks, turning me to face the wall and bending me slightly. "Hands on the wall," he orders, and I do it, mainly because I need him back inside me now. His mouth comes close to my ear as he impales me again. "If only you were always this compliant, Ten." He grips my hips and slams into me at a punishing pace. I cry out, struggling to stay upright as he fucks me hard and fast.

"You need to come, Ten," he pants, but I shake my head. I can't come from penetration, so it's fruitless him trying to wait for me. "What the fuck you talking about, no?" he growls. "Come, damn it."

"I can't," I hiss, resting my head to one side against the wall.

"The fuck you can't, Ten. Come," he demands again.

"Tag, I—" The protest dies on my lips as a sensation flurries inside my stomach. "Oh fuck," I mumble. It builds and builds until the energy zapping around my body makes me shake. I cry out and my legs go weak, but Tag holds me up. I've never felt an orgasm so intense, and as my body jerks and bucks against him, he whispers words of encouragement in my ear. I'm a panting, sweaty mess as I come down from the high. Tag doesn't stop, fucking me harder to chase his own release, which soon follows. He stiffens, roaring in pleasure.

"Ten, you surprise me with your amazingly hot body, and then you come on my cock and blow my fucking mind," he pants into my hair. "We need to do that again at least three more times." I glimpse back at him, realising he isn't joking. "Where's the bedroom?"

TAG

Sometimes, after the cards have gone out to random girls on my fight nights, I regret the game. I go over why we do it, what started it, and how it became such a bad habit that neither myself nor Anton seem to want to stop. But laying here, next to Ten, I don't regret Anton choosing her. He rated her a ten, but honestly, she's gone up in the ranks by a whole lot more. She's amazing, not just in bed—although she's great at that part too—but she isn't in awe of me, and I like that. She doesn't give a crap about the money, the flashy car, or being on my arm. I feel like she actually wants to get to know the real me, not the Tag that everyone else sees.

She stretches out beside me, and I catch another glimpse of her naked breast as the sheet slips down. If I could, I'd try for a fourth time, but it's the early hours of the morning and I'm exhausted. "Do you get on with your mum?" she mumbles, her eyes blinking sleepily.

"Most of the time. Sometimes we fight, but it's mainly because she's worried about me. She doesn't want me to take on my father's role."

"What was your father's role?"

"Running the family."

"Why doesn't she want you to do that?"

"In my world, it's dangerous. There are too many people watching your every move and waiting to take you down. She's scared I'll end up like him."

"Is that a bad thing?"

I nod. "Sort of. Tell me about your mum."

Lucy sighs. "She's spoilt, wants everything for nothing. I don't want to be like her. She says I take after my father, my real one, and that apparently isn't a good thing."

"What do you know about him?"

"Not a lot. He wasn't rich enough to keep my mum interested, which is sad really. You'd think she would have wanted a father for her child. She tells the story like he ran from commitment, but I know her and I know he was her bit of rough. Every rich girl wants a secret bad boy." She pauses for a beat, smirking at me. "I used to think he'd come and find us, because I really believed that she missed him. If we ever talked about him, which wasn't often, she'd get this longing in her eyes like she loved him so much that it hurt her to remember. He never came back, and she never went looking. When she met my stepfather, she refused to speak about him again. I guess she'd moved on to better things."

"Love's a funny thing."

"Have you ever been in love?" she asks, rolling onto her stomach and laying her head sideways, resting on her arms.

"No. Never."

"When we first met, you spoke like you loved someone."

"Did I? I don't remember. What does it feel like, Ten? Tell me what you feel when you're with Noah."

She sighs. "It wasn't instant. Like it wasn't love at first sight, if that's even a thing. I liked him. We were at college together and we used to see each other in the library, so we were both geeks. One day, we got talking and then he took me out and it just kind of snowballed. My mother loves him, mainly because he's from money. If anything happens to his father, he'll take over the entire firm. I wonder what that will be like though," she trails off.

"Him being Senior Partner of a huge law firm, I imagine it would be amazing but hard work."

"I never see him now. If he heads up the firm, I'll be one of those women who do lunch and spends her days getting her hair done or carrying a handbag-sized dog." She shudders. "It's not the life I want."

"You have your own business. You'd still have that."

"Noah hates my business. He talks like it's a game I play at to keep me occupied. When we marry, I think he might push me to sell it. It wouldn't look good if his wife is working, like he can't provide."

"Sounds like a pile of shit if you ask me. If you think that, why would you even consider marrying him?"

Lucy shrugs again and her eyes flutter closed. "I'm always wondering the same thing."

I wait for a few minutes until I hear her breathing deepen. Sliding from her bed, I dress quickly, making sure there's no trace of me left behind. I bury the waste at the bottom of the small bin beside the bed. I wouldn't want Mr. Perfect to find the used, discarded condoms. I take one last look at Lucy's sleeping form and then leave.

I call Tony, who answers on the first ring. "Thanks for waiting around, man. If you need to get off, I'm all done here." I had him follow that prick so I'd know if he was heading back here.

"I'm all good, boss. I'll follow you back to your apartment and then head off from there."

"Where'd her lover boy disappear to?" I ask.

"He met with a female. They had dinner and then he went to a hotel alone. An hour later, another female went to his room. The room was booked under his company name and they're still there now."

I get into my car, feeling bad for Lucy. Her boyfriend is a dog, cheating, lying, and treating her like shit. She deserves better, and I hate she'll wake up and feel guilty when he's doing the exact same thing to her.

Chapter Eleven

♥

LUCY

Sunday brunch with my mother has become a little too regular for my liking. It was only two weeks since we last did this, and now, I'm here again. And it's the last place I feel like being, seeing as I'm racked with guilt yet all I can think about is Tag and how good he made me feel.

"How would you feel if I was to go and look for my father?" I ask casually.

She stops stirring her green tea and looks at me with a blank expression. "Why?"

"Well, mainly because he's my father and I'd like to meet the man who made me."

"Why now?"

"Why not now?"

"Lucy, do you have to be so irritating? I don't need you to answer me with a question. You've never bothered before, so I'd like to know why the sudden interest."

"I don't know." I shrug. "I've just been thinking about him is all. If I marry Noah, I'd like my real father to be at my wedding. What if he has other children? They're my brothers and sisters."

My mother snorts in disgust. "I'm certain he would have had many other children. He was terrible at, how do I say it . . . keeping it in his pants."

"He cheated?"

"More than likely. I didn't stick around to find out. I wouldn't even know where to tell you to begin looking. Focus on your future, darling, he was bad news."

"If I still have a future. Noah and I had a huge fight last night. He walked out."

"Lucy, why do you insist on upsetting the apple cart? Men like Noah do not like a nagging woman. If you're not careful, he'll look elsewhere, just like his father has."

I glare at her. "Shh," I whisper, looking around. I told her about Emma and Clyde in confidence.

"I'm just saying that you need to support him more. You'll end up alone."

"I'm not an ugly old witch, Mother. I'll find another man if Noah decides to dump me."

"Noah is a good man and he can take care of you. Not many men are like him."

"Not everything is about money, Mother. There are other lovely men out there who aren't rich but are still amazing."

"You're losing your mind if you think a poor man from the East End is going to make you happy. Stop talking nonsense about finding your deadbeat father and leaving Noah for a poor man."

I roll my eyes at her dramatics. She never listens. "Can't you tell me anything about him?"

"No, and even if I could, I wouldn't because it's a waste of time. He cruised into my life on his big, shiny motorcycle and left the same way. He was more interested in his biker club than me and making a life. I thought he had money, but when it came down to it, he had nothing."

I don't push her any further on it. She's getting irate and upset, so I change the subject to something she loves—herself.

When I return home later, Noah is in the shower. "Is that you?" he shouts.

Chucking my keys on the side, I go through to the bedroom. The bathroom leads on from there, and the door is open with steam billowing out. "If you mean me as in Lucy, then yes. We need to talk."

"I don't like the sound of that," he replies.

Since waking up, all I've thought about is what I did. I've cheated and that breaks my heart, because despite our problems, Noah doesn't deserve my disloyalty. If I truly loved him, I wouldn't have done that, and it makes me question everything we have together. I watch as he comes into the bedroom, rubbing his hair vigorously on his towel. "Where did you stay last night?"

"In a hotel. I thought we needed time to cool down."

"I think we need a break, Noah," I say firmly. I've never suggested this before, and Noah looks surprised. "You lashed out again, and I'm sick of it. One night away doesn't make things better." I hate myself for using that as the main excuse, putting all the blame on him.

"What will our parents say?" he asks.

"That's all you've got? I suggest a break and you're worried about what our fucking parents will say?" I feel hurt that his first reaction wasn't to beg me to reconsider. "Just get your shit together and leave."

"Lucy, let's think about this. We're onto a good thing, me and you, and we have a big future together with a dream wedding and a fantastic lifestyle." He pulls on a pair of jeans, followed by a T-shirt.

"It's not my dream. It's yours, your parents', and my mother's. I want to be happy, and at the minute, I'm really not."

"Well, I think you're being dramatic. So, we argued, couples do that all the time."

I point to the bruises littering my neck. "I had to wear a fucking silk scarf today to cover this shit and I'm sick of it. I don't want to spend my life scared of what mood you're in or not being able to say what I feel. You haven't touched me in ages, unless you count the times you've lashed out, and I can't do it anymore. We're allowing the cycle of unhappy marriages to continue just because we're doing what our parents want. You don't love me, Noah."

"You're being dramatic. So, I got a little angry. You didn't exactly help in that."

"So, I deserved to be choked?" I snap. I note he didn't even bother to deny the fact I accused him of not loving me. I sigh. "Look, let's just take some time apart to decide what's best for us both."

"Right, and for how long?" I shrug, and he scoffs, shaking his head angrily. "Fine. But don't take too long, Lucy, I might get bored of waiting." He storms out the room without taking any of his belongings, and a few minutes later, I hear the front door slam.

I call Tyra, and she answers after two rings. "Girl, I feel like we're becoming strangers."

"Sorry, T, I've had a lot going on. Are you free to come over?"

"Of course. Is everything okay?"

"Yeah. Bring Bel if she's free."

The girls arrive in less than an hour armed with gin and chocolate. "You sounded weird on the phone, so I thought maybe it was either a crisis or that time of the month," explains Tyra, dumping the gin on the countertop in the kitchen. The girls take a seat at the breakfast bar, and I pull out three glasses.

"I wouldn't call it a crisis as such," I say, opening the gin and pouring it across the glasses. "I told Noah I want a break." I add some lemonade to each glass and hand them out.

The girls exchange a shocked look. "I wasn't expecting that. I was thinking pregnancy scare," says Tyra.

"Now, that would be a crisis," I groan. "And . . . last night, I cheated." I watch as those words register in their brains and then both gasp in surprise. "With Tag," I add for shock value.

"Jesus!" screeches Bel. "What the hell happened to you?"

"Calm down, Bel. I'm only human, and did you actually see Tag? I mean, you said yourself he was gorgeous."

"How did all of this happen without us knowing anything? You must have been sneaking around with him for ages and not told us a thing," says Tyra accusingly.

"He was turning up a lot, and I guess I fell for his charm." I shrug guiltily.

"You don't fall for charm, Lucy. I can count on you to not fall for the charm," yells Bel.

"I don't think it was his charm that got her, Bels." Tyra winks.

"So, are you with Tag now?" asks Bel.

"No," I gasp. "God, we only slept together once. Well, not once. Well, it was one night but lots of times," I explain, blushing.

"Oh man, I wanted him so bad. Was he good?" Tyra groans, and Bel playfully slaps her arm. "What? A girl's gotta know," she says innocently. I smirk, and Tyra screams excitedly, "You lucky bitch!"

"Are we just going to overlook the fact that she cheated?" Bel asks.

The guilt hits me again and I groan, burying my face in my hands. "I know, I'm an awful person, aren't I?"

"Bel, we don't even like Noah," Tyra reminds her. "I'm glad she's cheated. We all know he's probably done the same a million times over."

"Great, thanks, T," I mutter, rolling my eyes.

"Oh my god, you need to call Tag and see what's happening between the two of you," she goes on to say.

I shake my head. "No way," I protest. I gulp down my gin and pour another glass. "He snuck out of here before I woke this morning. He's probably regretting the whole thing. Besides, he's a one-night type of guy, isn't he? We all know his type." I smile wickedly. "But, boy, was it a good night." The girls fall about laughing.

TAG

I slam my fist against the punch bag, and as it rocks back towards me, I hit it again. I have another fight coming and there's a lot of money riding on it, so I need to get my head in the game. But I can't get Lucy off my mind. I keep picturing her soft pink lips all swollen from my kisses and the way she met me thrust for thrust.

It's been five days since that night and I've tried to keep away. My conscience is starting to get the better of me, and I'm trying to think of a way to tell Anton that I'm pulling the plug on our little game. It seems wrong to make her fall for me knowing I have no intentions of pursuing her for real. She's got enough going on with her abusive prick of a boyfriend.

Anton is watching from outside the ring. "You look uptight. Everything okay?"

I hit the bag a few more times before resting my head against it. I squeeze my eyes closed. "We haven't played the game for a while. Bring the cards tonight."

"Thought you didn't want to play the game now the stakes were set higher?"

"Maybe the stakes are too high. Maybe I've grown a fucking conscience, which is as surprising to me as it is to you."

"Piss off." He laughs, jumping up from his seat and striding over to the ringside. "She sent you packing, didn't she, which means I won."

"She didn't send me anywhere," I mutter, wishing she had.

"We have a deal, Tag. No backing out, man."

"Come on, Anton, you're not that cruel. It's different when we don't know them. It's easier. But she's nice, man, and she's got shit going on."

"Tag, I don't give a fuck what she's got going on. A deal is a deal, unless you want to make me the winner, and that means signing over your apartment and walking away from Ella . . . for good."

Ella. Fucking Ella. I groan as Anton leaves the ringside, his laughter echoing around the gym. Letting him win means I won't hear the end of it. And losing Ella . . . can I lose her? I growl, slamming my fists into the bag.

I won the fight, of course, and as I enter the top floor of the hotel, which we often rent out for the afterparty, I realise I'm not looking forward to it. I'm the first to throw a party, any excuse will do, but tonight, I'm not feeling the right vibes.

It's the same faces—men from our organization, women on their arms who look far too young for them and are definitely not their wives. Anton passes me a shot glass overflowing with an amber liquid. The sticky fluid spills over the glass and drips down my hand. I knock it back because it's what I'm expected to do, but the usual buzz is gone.

"What's up with your face, bro? You won, so where's the happiness?"

I sigh. "I'm not feeling it, Ant."

"Jesus, stop mooning over that chick. If I knew you were gonna turn into a pussy, I'd have agreed to play the game tonight. In fact . . ." He looks around the room and his eyes settle on a blonde standing out on the balcony with her friend. "She's a ten. Go play."

I look her over. "Not ten. Eight maybe, but not ten."

"Tag, stop. Are we never gonna say the word 'ten' again because you got your panties in a twist over some whore?"

I react without thinking, shoving Anton up against the nearest wall and growling in his face. "She's not a damn whore!"

Anton smirks, and as I remember my place, I take a step back, feeling eyes on us. Anton signals that he's okay as his minder steps forward. "You do remember why you started all this, right?" He waits a beat, and when I don't reply, he steps closer, lowering his voice. "You started the whole fucking thing, Tag. You want my sister, then you show me how far you're willing to go for her, and if you don't want her anymore, I want a good fucking reason not to kill you for turning your nose up at her."

"I can't fuck up her life, man. She's a nice girl."

"I didn't ask you to fuck up her life. No one said ruin her. The deal was to make her fall for you. When did all this shit become so serious?"

"Fucking with someone's life is serious. We need to grow the fuck up," I growl.

"If I didn't know better, I'd say you were falling for Ten." Anton grins and cocks his eyebrow before adding, "And where does that leave my sister?"

"I love your sister, you know I do. I guess Ten is just . . ." I trail off, not knowing what Ten is anymore.

"Well, here's your chance to find out." I turn to the direction he's nodding. When my eyes fall upon Ten, I inhale sharply, feeling my throat tighten and an unusual pain pull at my heart.

She looks hot in tight denim and a black top. Her heels click on the marble floor as she heads towards me, flicking her long brown hair over her shoulder. Her two friends are following behind, but as she reaches me, she looks me up and down before continuing on past me. Her friends smirk, and I'm left open-mouthed and confused.

"What the fuck is she doing here, Anton?"

He holds up my mobile phone and grins wide, opening the screen and flicking over it with his finger. "So, you think you can just fuck me and then disappear?" he reads out loud before I snatch it from him. Sure enough, she texted me an hour ago, and Anton responded with the hotel details, pretending to be me. "Why the fuck she'd come after how you've treated her screams desperation, Tag," he mutters in my ear, and it irritates me. For the second time this evening, I want to punch his smug face. Instead, I follow after her.

"Ten," I say to her retreating back. She stops, as do her friends, and she turns to me, a scowl firmly in place.

"My name," she hisses, "is Lucy."

"Lucy," I correct. "Can we please talk?"

"No," she snaps, going to walk away again. This time, I grab her arm, and instead of yelling at me, which I fully expect, she flinches away from me, a terrified expression on her face. Even her friends notice her reaction and shift uncomfortably. I decide to avoid an embarrassing confrontation and lift her easily, flinging her over my shoulder. She screams and then hits me in the back. I grin as her tiny fists bounce off me, knowing it must hurt her more than it does me.

The crowd parts as I march with a purpose towards the bedroom. Once inside, I lower her to the ground, and she folds her arms over her chest, defiance on her face. "How dare you—" she begins, but I cut her off, pressing my body against hers until she's backed up against the wall.

"I missed your mouth," I growl.

"Not enough to pick up the phone?" she retorts.

I smirk and then press my lips against hers, hoping a toe-curling kiss will change her frosty mood. I feel her hands pushing at my shoulders and, eventually, she turns her head away. "No," she hisses. "No, you can't fuck your way out of this."

"Out of what? I haven't done anything."

"It's not okay to act like you did and then go radio silent on me for a week."

"You haven't texted me either," I point out, and she scowls again.

"I didn't want to appear desperate," she offers feebly.

"And turning up here was you appearing cool and relaxed?" I laugh, and she shoves past me, heading for the door to leave. "Come on, Luce, I'm sorry," I say, catching her by the hand and pulling her back to me. "You're not leaving here until you stop being mad."

"Then we could be here a while." I love that she's calling me out on my bullshit.

I pull her towards the bed and sit while she stands before me. "All I have is time, baby," I say, wiggling my brows. I see a small smile appear on her lips, but she shuts it down quickly. "Anyway, I have some news for you."

"Oh?" she asks, curiosity taking over her mood.

"Yeah, you mentioned you wanted to trace your father. Well, I know someone who can help with that."

She frowns. "How? Who?"

"All you have to do is give me the nod and I'll have him look into it." I leave out the part that I discovered who her father was last night when my guy contacted me. Luckily, I know of him, and he's not all that bad, but I can see why her mother didn't want to stick with him. Being in the MC lifestyle takes a certain kind and rich bitches have no place there.

"Well, if you think you can, but I have nothing to go on."

"I don't need anything but your name, sweetheart, and that, I already have."

"So, where have you been all week?"

"Training, business, more training."

"Did you win tonight?"

"Of course. Did you doubt me?"

I tug her again, and she falls on top of me. I wrap my arms around her waist and go in for another kiss. This time, she allows it, and before long, I have her flipped underneath me, my hands roaming her tight little body as she squirms with impatience. "You know how many times I've had to touch myself this week, thinking about you?" She shakes her head, biting her lower lip. "A lot."

"Maybe I can give your hand a rest." She smirks, tugging at the button on my jeans. I look down between us, watching as she frees my erection.

"I think that sounds like a good plan." I roll onto my back so I'm beside her. She gets onto her knees and tugs the jeans down my hips until I'm fully exposed to her. I prop my head up using a pillow so I can watch her. She fists my cock, pumping until a bead of cum drips down the head. Smiling, she flicks out her tongue, catching it in one quick sweep. She licks her lips and then runs her tongue up the shaft of my erection. It jerks in her hands, and I let out a sharp hiss. I've been thinking about a moment just like this all week. When she finally takes me into her hot mouth, I let my head fall back in ecstasy. This chick is blowing my mind.

Chapter Twelve

♥

LUCY

I roll over, hitting against a hot, hard body. Opening one eye, I remember exactly where I am and a smile forms on my lips. It feels good to wake up next to Tag. "What are you smiling about?" he grumbles sleepily.

"How do you know I'm smiling?" I ask, laying on my side and propping my head up on my hand. He reaches out and gently tugs my nipple, sending a bolt of electricity straight to my pussy.

"I heard it." He smiles, opening his eyes.

I laugh. "You can't hear a smile," I insist. He leans forwards, taking the erect nipple into his mouth and humming his approval. "Did I mention I'm free all day?" I grin, running my fingers through his hair.

"Oh yeah? Is lover boy at work again?" he asks, turning his attention to my other nipple.

"About that," I say slowly, "Noah and I kind of split up." Tag freezes. I feel his whole body tense up, and then he pulls back.

"What?" he asks, his face suddenly serious. I miss his playful expression from just moments ago.

"I thought that would be a good thing," I mumble.

"Why did you split up?"

"Erm, well, a few reasons, but one of them being you," I say, sitting up and wrapping the sheet around my naked form. Suddenly, I feel exposed and vulnerable. I watch as Tag swings his legs over the edge of the bed, and he leans his elbows on his knees, putting his head in his hands.

"Fuck, Ten, why'd yah have to ruin it?" He groans, and this time, my body tenses.

"Ruin what?"

"This," he snaps, turning to glare at me, waving a hand between us both. "We had a good little thing going and then you go and do that."

"I don't understand. I thought you'd be pleased."

"Well, you thought wrong. Get dressed and get the fuck out of here."

He says it with such venom in his voice that it causes a physical pain in my chest. I rub the sore spot, looking around the room for my clothes. Without a word, I get out of the bed and scoop my clothes from a pile on the floor. Thank God I didn't throw them around in a fit of passion.

Locking myself in the en-suite, I dress quickly. I'm so confused by his sudden change in behaviour that I don't really think about anything but getting out of here with as much dignity as I can muster. I look myself over in the brightly-lit mirror. Wiping a finger under each eye, I rid myself of last night's makeup. Standing straight, I jut out my chin and square my shoulders. Fuck Tag and his gorgeous body. Fuck him and his 'come to bed' eyes. And fuck him and his great fucking. I can do better.

I swoop through the bedroom, not bothering to look in his direction. "Ten, wait," he calls out. I'm already pulling the door open, but I feel his force slam it shut, blocking my escape. "I said wait," he snaps.

"I want to leave," I mutter, keeping my back to him.

"The condom split," he mumbles. I turn to face him, and he holds up the used condom. "I thought I felt it, but I've only just checked it. It's split."

"I'll take care of it," I tell him, tugging at the door handle again while repeating 'fuck' over and over in my head. This is the last thing I need right now.

"I'd prefer to come with you to the pharmacy, to make sure . . ." He trails off, and I try to ignore the insult. After all, he doesn't know me well, and he must meet people wanting to trap him all the time.

"I'll video it," I snap.

"Lucy, please, this is important."

Tears well in my eyes and I inwardly curse. I don't want him to see me upset, so I turn the heartbreak into anger. "Really, because a second ago, you couldn't wait to get rid of me. Now, you want me to wait so you can accompany me to the damn pharmacy? I don't want to spend another second with you, Tag, let alone get lumbered with your kid. So, trust me when I say, I'll take care of this."

He's not going to budge, his expression determined. "It'll take half an hour and then you'll be rid of me. You can stand there with a bad attitude and a sassy mouth, but I'm coming with you, so accept it."

I weigh up my options. He's the type to throw me in the boot and take me anyway. I huff, so he knows that I'm not happy. "Fine, I'll wait out there for you," I say coldly. He releases his hold on the door, and I stomp past him, elbowing him in the stomach for good measure as I pass. A feeling of satisfaction washes over me when I hear him groan.

I step into the large living area. It's a huge room, taking the whole top floor of the hotel. There's a group of men sitting around the kitchen table playing a game of cards. A pile of money sits in the middle and a cloud of cigar smoke lingers above their heads. I don't think they've bothered to go to bed. I recognise one of the men as Anton, Tag's friend. Next to him is Ella.

She spots me and saunters over. She's wearing a man's white shirt that's open to almost between her breasts. She folds her arms and the shirt rides up her slender, tanned thighs. "Good night?" she asks, arching her perfect brow.

"Yes, thank you."

"Are you sure? You look upset."

"I'm fine."

"I know he's a handful and all . . ." She leaves that statement in the air and it feels like a claim to him. She twists a lock of hair around her finger, her perfectly manicured nail glimmering in the light. "Do you like him?"

"I don't even know who you are, so I'm hardly going to talk about my private life with you," I say, feeling annoyed by her presence.

She covers her mouth in mock horror and laughs. "Oh my god, you do. You like Tag Corallo." She reminds me of the bullies at school who would make others feel shit for breathing the same air. A mean girl.

"And it's your business because?" I snap.

"You know who he is, right?" she asks, narrowing her eyes and looking me up and down. "You think someone of his stature, a mafia boss, would ever go for someone like you? He likes me because I'm pure, saving myself especially for our wedding night."

My heart hammers wildly in my chest and there's a whooshing sound in my ears. "What are you talking about?"

"You're just a game to him, a chance for him to win a bet with my brother." She tips her head to one side and pouts out her bottom lip. "I feel sorry for you, but Tag wants me, and to get me, he needs my brother's help. If Tag could get you to fall for him, my brother promised to put in a good word with my father. You're a means to an end, and by the state of you, it looks like he's won." She winks before turning on her heel and sauntering back to the table, settling next to her brother, who's watching me closely.

I inhale sharply, the pain in my chest too much. I need air. I rush to the elevator and push the button several times. After what seems like hours, it pings open, and I sigh in relief as I step inside and push for the ground floor. I see Tag come out of the bedroom just as the doors begin to close. His eyes lock with mine and then he runs towards me, but it's too late. The doors slide closed and the elevator begins its decent.

My mind races. What the hell was that? I want to believe that it isn't true, but why would she lie to me? I picture her smug face as those words spilled from her mouth. My mobile buzzes in my bag and I pull it free to see Tag's name flashing up. I cancel the call. The elevator opens and I rush out of the hotel, breaking out into the fresh air to take deep, calming breaths. The street is quiet with just the odd weekend runner passing by. A cab pulls up, dropping off a businessman, and as soon as he steps out, I dive in and ask the driver to take me to Tyra's place. If anyone knows the truth about Tag, it'll be her.

When I arrive a few minutes later, I press the call button for Tyra's apartment. It takes me several attempts before her sleepy voice crackles through the intercom. I sigh in relief. "Ty, it's Luce. Let me up," I say.

I find Tyra leaning against her kitchen counter, her head in her hands and the coffee pot making a gurgling sound as it comes to life. "What the hell sort of time do you call this?"

"Ty, what do you know about Tag?" I ask, and she uncovers her face and frowns at me.

"You woke me up at this ungodly hour to ask about lover boy?" she growls.

"It's really important," I say, desperation in my voice. "I just had a run-in with his friend's sister. She said some shit that I can't get my head around."

Tyra moves to the coffee machine and fills two mugs. She passes me one and we head into the living room and take a seat on her over-sized couch. "Okay, start from the beginning," she prompts.

"He told me this chick is really into him and that he goes along with it because he doesn't want to upset her father, that he'd kill him. I didn't think he was serious, but this morning, she told me that Tag was some kind of Mafia boss. Is that true?"

"There are rumours that he's in with the Mafia, but come on, Luce, how much of that is really true? That stuff's in movies. He's probably getting a bad reputation because of his MMA stuff, and maybe he's in some sort of crime ring?"

"But why would she say that? She told me Tag is using me to win a bet with her brother, that he's doing it to win her father's approval. I mean, that shit sounds Mafia to me."

"Has he ever given you any reason to think he's not one hundred percent into you?"

I think for a moment and then shake my head. "Not until today." I sigh.

"Then I wouldn't worry. Maybe she's just a crazed fan or something. You know how girls get over gorgeous men."

"I caught him roughing up a restaurant owner once."

"Right, so that means he must be a Mafia boss," scoffs Tyra, rolling her eyes. "Besides, he wouldn't be doing the dirty work himself if he was a big boss. He'd have soldiers for that."

"Maybe. But that gives me an idea. We could go and ask the restaurant owner?"

"We?" repeats Tyra, raising her eyebrows.

"You're a journalist. Maybe you could get a big story out of all this." I look into the distance. "Journalist uncovers London Mafia!" I spread my hands out like I'm revealing the headline, and Tyra grins wide. I don't tell her that if the story is true, we might be in danger. I doubt the Mafia would like their shit exposed all over *The London Gazette*.

"Let me get dressed." She rushes to her bedroom enthusiastically.

I pull out my mobile while I wait. There's a text message from Tag telling me that he's at my apartment and I need to hear him out. I contemplate texting back, but the stubborn bitch in me refuses to engage in conversation until I know what's lies and what's not.

When we arrive at the restaurant, it's closed. We go around the back, where we find a teenage boy smoking a cigarette. He eyes us suspiciously. "We're looking for the owner."

"Why?"

"It's really important. Tell him we're friends of Tag," says Tyra coolly.

The teenager looks cautious and flicks his cigarette before going inside. "Great, you've scared him off," I hiss. "Why'd yah mention Tag?"

I'm turning to leave when the back door opens again and the owner steps out. "Who are you?" he snaps.

I turn and offer a small smile. "Hey, I'm Lucy. I came here with Tag a few weeks ago. He roughed you up."

"What of it?"

"I just had a question for you and I was hoping you could help me. Tag doesn't know I'm here."

He looks around suspiciously and then opens the door wider for us to go inside. The back room is dark and dirty. A wooden table sits against the wall with a few stools placed around it. We sit down, but the guy remains standing, like he wants to bolt out of here. "You know what he'd do if he caught you sneaking around behind his back asking questions?" he asks, sticking a cigarette into his mouth and lighting it.

"What would he do?" asks Tyra.

"If you know him like you say you do, then you'd already know the answer to that."

"Actually," I cut in, "that's why I'm here. I thought I knew him pretty well, but I think he's been hiding things from me, like who he actually is."

"And you thought by coming here, I'd confess all?" He laughs, blowing smoke from his mouth and then coughing violently.

"How much money do you owe him?" I ask.

He scowls at me. "Too much."

"I'll pay it off, all of it, if you tell me what I want to know." That wasn't my original plan, but I didn't expect this to be such hard work.

"I'm not being rude, but you have no idea what you're asking of me."

"It won't go any further than this room," I say, my tone begging.

"My friend just needs to know how far she should run from Tag," says Tyra, and I know by her tone that she isn't taking this seriously at all.

"Far . . . as far as she can," he says coldly. "And when you think you're far enough, run a little more."

"I was told he's some kind of boss in a gang."

He laughs, shaking his head. "Jesus, you have no idea."

"So, he's a Mafia boss?" asks Tyra, almost laughing. Her smile fades when the guy stares her down.

"You think this is a joke? That these men don't exist? I bet you lay your pretty little head on your soft white pillow every night dreaming of unicorns and girly nights out drinking Champagne." He sneers but continues. "The rest of us skulk around in the shadows trying not to be seen by men like him, sleeping with one eye open in case they turn up to kill my family in their sleep. Tag isn't fussy—he'll put a bullet in my wife's head before my eyes if it means he's a step closer to becoming his father."

I exchange a look with Tyra and then rise to my feet. "That's all I needed to know, thanks."

"The truth isn't pretty, is it? Whatever you were told about him was probably true. If you want to keep dreaming of unicorns, then stay the hell away from him. Him and Anton."

"His friend?" I ask, and he nods.

"Anton is the son of *the* boss. A lethal fucker who would smile while slitting your throat. Then there's his sister, the apple of his father's eye but just as fucked-up."

I head for the door, followed closely by Tyra. "I'll be back in touch about the money," I add before leaving.

Chapter Thirteen

TAG

"I want her found now," I hiss into my phone then disconnect the call with Tony. I pace the hotel room again. Lucy has disappeared. She wasn't at her apartment, and Antonio can't track her mobile.

"What's the big deal?" whines Ella sulkily. She wasn't happy that I yelled when she confessed to shooting her mouth off to Lucy.

"Did you do it so your brother wins the bet?" I snap.

She flinches. "No."

"The condom split," I hiss, and Ella rears back like I've slapped her. "And now, she might not take the morning after pill as one last fuck you!"

"Then you need to find her," she yells, standing.

"What do you think I'm trying to do?" I ask through gritted teeth, running my fingers through my tousled hair in frustration. I begin to pace again.

Anton joins us after seeing the men out. "What's going on?"

"Your sister here opened her big mouth and told Ten about the bet."

Anton looks at Ella, and she shrugs. "So?" he replies.

"So . . ." I turn my back to him, unable to find the right words. Finding out she dumped that piece of shit made what I've done to her all the more real. I've fucked her life up completely, and now, she's single, alone, and her future plans of marriage and a life have been messed up. I hate how the guilt is ripping me up inside. And now, she's walked out of here knowing about our seedy fucking bet, possibly with my kid planted in her stomach. I groan out loud. It's a clusterfuck, and there's no one to blame but myself.

My phone beeps, and when I see Lucy's name, I almost cheer with relief. I open the text and frown at the words.

Lucy: It's best we cut ties, Tag. Thanks for the fun times, but I'm out.

I rub the pain in my chest and bite my lower lip to stop the frustrated growl I feel building up. I should be relieved that she's doing the right thing, but I don't. The thought of never seeing her again is worse than the guilt I feel. And I'm not used to feeling anything, so I don't know what to do with the rollercoaster of emotion tearing me up.

"Is that her?" asks Ella, and I nod. "Are you going to take her to get the pill?" Her voice is irritating me, so I ignore her.

Tag: What about the morning after pill?

Lucy: I'd never tie myself to you permanently. You're not all that. I'll take the damn pill.

I don't doubt it. She's not the kind to trap me, but I have this niggling thought in my head telling me to go and see her one last time. I want to be sure there are no loose ends . . . or maybe I just want to torture myself one last time.

Tag: I need to know you've taken it. Meet me at the pharmacy on the high street in twenty minutes.

I head for the door, grabbing my car keys. "Where are you going?" asks Ella.

"I need to not be near you right now," I snap, leaving.

A short time later, I'm waiting in my car across the street from the pharmacy, tapping my fingers impatiently against the steering wheel. It's been twenty minutes exactly when I see her walking up the street. She stops outside the pharmacy, folding her arms across her chest. I step out of the car, putting my shades in place, and head over the road towards where she stands. I don't speak to her as I head inside, pushing the door hard and waiting for her to follow me. I approach the counter and lift my shades onto my head. "We need the morning after pill," I say to the assistant.

"Okay, follow me," she says, and we go into a side room. I lower into a chair and notice Lucy pulls the other chair farther away before sitting. I roll my eyes.

The assistant goes through some personal questions to Lucy. I pull out my phone and pretend to take no notice as she reels off her answers. The fact that she confesses to taking this pill more than once annoys me.

The assistant gives the pill to Lucy, and she swallows it down in one, giving me a hard stare while she gulps some water from a bottle. She turns to me and opens her mouth wide, lifting her tongue so I can see it's gone. "Enough," I growl, annoyed at her childish antics.

We leave after I've paid the bill, stepping out into the fresh, crisp air. Lucy goes to walk away, but I grab her arm and march her towards my car. I didn't plan on a little reunion, but my cool is dissolving by the second and the need to talk to her is overwhelming.

I open the passenger side and shove her into the seat. "Stay put. If you get back out of this car, I'll tie you up." Lucy's face pales slightly, and I wonder how much Ella actually told her about me. I get into the driver's side and start the engine. I don't have a clue where to take her—I just know she needs to hear me out.

We drive in silence to the small apartment I own in Knightsbridge. I stay here when I need to escape it all. No one knows about it, not even Anton. We drive into the underground car park. "Where are we?" she snaps.

"My apartment," I answer, and she mutters something to herself that I don't quite catch.

I turn to look at her for an explanation, and she scowls at me. "Well, it all makes sense now that I actually know. The apartments, the big hotels . . . god, I'm such an idiot."

I choose not to reply, because what can I say? I go around to the passenger side and pull her from the car, and she fights me, pulling her arm free but following me nonetheless. We step into the small elevator, and I resist the urge to kiss her. The pull is so strong, I have to squeeze my fists into balls, knowing she'll lose her mind if I try anything right now.

Unlocking the apartment door, I step aside so she can go in first, not wanting to risk her running. She looks around. It's smaller than my other apartment, but it's just right for one person. "I really don't want to hear what you've got to say."

"Yet here you are. Sit," I order, pointing to the couch. I can see that she's torn. She wants to tell me to piss off, but she's warring with herself. "Say it," I push. "You would have said it before you knew."

"It's different now I know," she snaps. "You might slit my throat."

"Maybe," I mutter. "Then I can go on living my life knowing that no one else can have you."

She raises her eyebrows and shifts uncomfortably before taking a seat. "Fucking psycho," she almost whispers. "Why me?" she asks, and it pulls at the heart strings that I didn't know existed before now. And I know without a doubt, I owe her the truth.

"Wrong place, wrong time. You challenged me when you pushed me away. I had to have you to prove a point."

"The numbers on the cards?"

"A different challenge. A stupid game. Anton gives score cards out to the women I have to chase. I do the same to him. The points add to our monthly score, and whoever has the most points in the end, wins."

"Where did I come on the scale?" she asks coldly, and I sigh.

"The scale is to twenty."

"Wow, I was a halfway score. Why didn't you go for twenty instead of my measly ten?"

"I did," I admit. "First." A look crosses Lucy's face, like she's been sucker punched. "Sometimes we sleep with lots of different girls in a night. More points that way. You caught my eye."

"Lucky me," she mumbles.

"If it makes a difference, I argued that you should have been higher, but number ten was the last card left when Anton saw you. Then you turned me down and I was intrigued. I stupidly upped the stakes, telling Anton that I could get you to fall for me if he would back me with his father."

"You know how childish this all sounds, right?" she snaps, standing. I tower over her. She isn't leaving yet, I'm not ready.

"Sit. Down," I say firmly. She lowers again, swallowing hard.

"So, what Ella said is true? Anton was backing you for her father's approval?"

I nod, feeling ashamed. "Yes, so I can marry her." As soon as the words leave my mouth, I regret them. It's the truth, and she deserves that, but it hurts us both. "It wasn't supposed to go this far. I wanted to pull out when I realised how nice you were, but it was too late and Anton wouldn't let me." She remains quiet, her eyes full of hate.

"That's why I was so annoyed that you'd ended things with your boyfriend. I didn't want to ruin your life."

"Don't flatter yourself, Tag. I didn't dump him so I could be with you. I just realised that if I was looking elsewhere, then Noah and I weren't meant to be."

"So, you didn't fall for me?" I ask.

She scoffs. "Jesus, you really are an egotistical prick. Would it make you feel better if I admit it? Then you can run along to your dickhead friend and tell him you won? Fine, Tag, you fucking won your bet."

Her words feel like punches. "I'm sorry, Lucy. I really am."

"Was any of it real?" she asks.

I nod. "More than I should have allowed," I admit.

"Is it true? Are you part of the Mafia?" I don't bother to answer her. What would it achieve?

"You should go and find that boyfriend of yours and sort shit out."

She shakes her head. "No, I'm done there. I'm going to enjoy being single for a while. Noah really wasn't a nice person. I seem to be a magnet for idiots."

"You deserve better, Lucy. I really am sorry. But look, if you ever need anything, I'm always just a call away." She laughs, but it's cold. Then she opens up her mobile and proceeds to delete my number, showing me the screen.

"If I ever need anything, you're the last person on the earth I'd ever call. I don't want anything to do with you. Stay away from me."

She rises to her feet, and this time, I let her. As she heads for the door, I say, "Just one thing before you go." I pull out a piece of paper and hold it out to her. "In case you wanted to know, this is your father, your real one. If you don't want it, just throw it away, but I thought you should at least have the opportunity to know who he is. He's a good guy, I know of him."

She takes the paper and holds it tight in her hands. "You found him for me?"

I shrug like it was nothing. "I have contacts," I joke, but she doesn't smile.

"And you know him?"

"I know of him. He's a decent guy, and I'm pretty sure it wouldn't have been him who left you out of choice. He's big on family."

As she passes me to leave, I link my fingers with hers, halting her. "Goodbye, Lucy," I whisper, and she looks up, her eyes full of sadness. She stands on her tiptoes and places a gentle kiss against the side of my mouth. I savour it, closing my eyes. They remain closed long after she pulls away, and I don't open them until I hear the sound of the door open and close.

LUCY

It's been a whole week since I last saw Tag after the pharmacy incident. It's not been easy, and as I sit waiting for Penelope, I think back to the address that Tag gave me for my real father. I haven't done anything with it yet. If I contact him, I'm opening all kinds of old wounds, especially for my mum, and I don't know how my stepfather would react.

Penelope enters the restaurant gracefully. She reminds me of my mother in some ways, which makes her the perfect wife for Wyatt. I stand as she approaches the table, and we air-kiss. "It's been so long since I last heard from you," she says coolly, shrugging out of her jacket and placing it carefully on the back of her chair.

"I've had a lot going on," I lie. Since she stomped out of my shop and accused Noah of having an affair, I've given her a bit of space.

"So I hear. Sleeping with rough boys behind your boyfriend's back," she says, taking her seat and finally looking me in the eye. I shift uncomfortably. If she's heard, then my mother must have, which would explain why she's been calling my mobile a lot this last week.

"That's not what I meant. Besides, you thought he was cheating on me anyway so—"

The waiter comes over to take our order, and as usual, Penelope orders salmon and new potatoes. I opt for a steak and ask for a bottle of house red. "I saw Noah. He's in bits," she says casually.

"You know how he treated me. I'm sure you weren't surprised when you heard we'd split up."

"I wasn't, I expected it, but I'd have liked to have heard it straight from you rather than him."

I sigh. "I was going to tell you, but things got in the way. I'm sorry, Pen."

"Tell me about this other man," she says, the beginnings of a smile showing.

"There's nothing to tell. We were never a thing. I got carried away, but he wasn't that into me. A good thing came from it all, though, because I realised Noah wasn't what I wanted."

"He told me that you were just on a break and that you'd get back together and marry like you've always planned." I shudder at the thought. "But actually, I found out something about Noah and I think I should tell you."

The waiter returns with my bottle of wine and pours us each a glass. "Go on," I urge.

"I was right about him cheating," she begins, a cautious tone to her voice. I wasn't expecting that, and I pick up my wine and gulp a mouthful. "I thought long and hard about whether I should tell you this, Lucy. It's really hard for me because it puts me right in the middle, but today I discovered something huge, and I really don't feel I should keep it a secret."

"You're scaring me, Pen," I mutter.

"It was Francesca," she almost whispers. I stare at her for some time, my mouth opening and closing. "When Noah said he intended on getting back together with you, I couldn't not tell you. You deserve so much better than him."

"Fran," I repeat. "It was Fran?" I think back to her reaction when Penelope accused Noah of having an affair. She was just as outraged as me.

"I'm so sorry, sweetie. I wanted to tell you as soon as I heard, but then you didn't return my calls . . ." I glare at her, and she trails off.

"Oh my god, does Gabs know?"

"She does now," she admits. "Fran told her because she found out something bigger."

"Bigger than her shagging my boyfriend?" I almost yell, and Penelope hisses at me to lower my voice.

"She's pregnant."

I put my head in my hands and groan. "Jesus," I mumble. My heart hurts, I feel so betrayed. How can one of my closest friends sleep with my boyfriend and then the rest of the group keep it from me?

"She doesn't know what to do. She's in turmoil."

"Seriously, should I call her and give her advice?" I ask sarcastically.

"Luce, you split up."

"That's not the point and you damn well know it," I hiss, grabbing my handbag from the floor. "You're all supposed to be my friends," I add. "I can't believe you all kept it from me and then you act like I should be sympathetic towards her."

"Please don't leave, not like this," she begs, and I roll my eyes. As if I'd stay and carry on like normal after hearing that. I chuck a twenty on the table to cover my meal, leaving Penelope to pay for the wine. It's the least she can do.

Outside, I flag a cab and jump in. I pull out the crumpled piece of paper and read the address to the driver. He turns to face me. "You sure, sweetheart?" he asks, and I nod. It's now or never.

Chapter Fourteen

LUCY

The cab slows outside a set of tall metal gates. The building behind is set right back and it's hard to make out if anyone is about. I pay the driver and step out. It's on an industrial estate, and because it's past eight in the evening, everywhere else on the estate is closed-up. I approach the gates, pushing on them to find them locked. I shake them again and they rattle.

"What do you want?" asks a gruff voice. I jump back in fright as a shadow of a man appears on the other side of the gates.

"Sorry, I'm looking for someone. Ace?"

"And who's asking?"

"Lucy. Lucy Clifford."

He disappears into a small gatehouse and then returns a few minutes later. "He says he don't know you."

"No, he doesn't, not really." I pause before adding, "I'm his daughter. Tell him I'm Sylvia's daughter."

"Okay, but I ain't making promises." He sighs and heads back into his gatehouse. A minute later, the gates clank and then begin to open. I let out a sigh of relief and step through. The man from the gatehouse is huge, and as I get closer, I notice that his face is disfigured. I look away before he notices me staring, keeping my eyes downwards.

"I'm Scar," he grunts, holding out his huge hand for me to shake. I do so, offering a smile. "I know it ain't pretty, but you can look."

I glance up. "Sorry, I was trying not to be rude."

"It's not rude, 'course people are curious." I follow him towards the building. As we get closer, I hear laughter and loud voices. "We're having a party, so it's busy in there. Ignore the fucking and shit. It gets crazy when the guys are drunk."

As we go inside, my eyes widen. He wasn't kidding when he said it'd be busy. There are men all around in leather jackets just like the one Scar is wearing. There's a huge skull on the back and the words 'The Rebellion MC' in large letters.

Hanging off most of the men are sexy women. I can't spot one plain-looking female in this place. "Follow me," says Scar, pushing his way through the crowd.

The room is huge, a warehouse which has been turned into a living space. We come to a standstill outside a black door with the word 'President' painted onto it. Scar knocks loudly and a second later we're told to enter. Butterflies have taken to fluttering around my stomach, and I suddenly feel sick with nerves. I'm about to meet my real father, a man I believed left us because he didn't care.

I follow Scar inside, where a large, handsome man maybe a few years older than me is scowling at me. He also wears a leather jacket with a skull and the words 'Vice President' are sewn onto his badge. He steps to one side as another man approaches. This guy is a lot older, with greying hair and piercing blue eyes very similar to my own. "Lucy," he utters, his brows drawn together like he can't quite believe it's me. I nod and smile, feeling the other guy's eyes burning into me.

"Thanks, Scar. Make sure we aren't disturbed," growls the younger of the two. Scar leaves, and even though I don't know him, I feel like I want him to stay. He was the barrier between us all. "Sit," the guy orders, glaring at me.

"Chill out, Hulk. You're gonna scare the poor girl," snaps the older guy. He smiles at me and then gestures for me to sit on a worn leather couch. I move slowly and then take a seat. "I'm Ace," he introduces, holding out his hand. I shake it, my small hand looking lost in his huge one. "How did you find me?"

"A friend," I say.

"What friend?" snaps Hulk.

"Not a friend, really." I sigh. "His names Tag. He's an MMA fighter."

"You mean Matteo Corallo?" Ace grins, sitting down on his office chair behind his desk. I nod, relieved that he seems to like Tag and not hate him. "I like that guy. Only met a handful of times, but he's straight talking, and I like that."

"And a mobster," snaps Hulk, huffing in disgust.

"I was hoping you'd come and find me one day," says Ace, ignoring Hulk's comment. "I spent a long time praying for you to come, especially once you'd turned eighteen and I knew your mother couldn't stop you. Does she know you're here?"

I shake my head. "She isn't keen on me finding you. I didn't even know I was coming here tonight. I just kind of hopped in a cab and decided."

"I'm so glad you did." He looks genuinely pleased to see me, and I feel a little more relaxed. "Your mother was never keen on me staying in contact. It eventually became too hard." He pauses and then shrugs. "But she was trying to do right by her baby, and I get that."

"Were you together?" I ask. I've only ever heard my mother's version, and she's one to stretch the truth to make herself look better.

Ace laughs, his head falling back and the sound vibrating off the walls. "God, no, she hated me. Actually, that's not strictly true. She liked me, a lot, but she came from a different background. She wanted to keep her parents happy and being with a biker was not on her agenda, or theirs for that matter. She didn't tell me she was pregnant, but I found out. I tried to get her to see sense, let me prove I'd make her happy, but she'd made her mind up that she wanted nothing to do with me. She let me see you a handful of times in secret, whenever she could get away, but the last time I saw you, you were a toddler and she told me the contact had to stop."

"She's stubborn," I say, smiling to show I don't mean it in a cruel way.

He smirks, like he's picturing her memory. "That she was." He falls silent for a moment and then looks towards where Hulk is stood awkwardly. "Shit, sorry, man." He stands and then smiles at me. "I didn't introduce you."

"Preoccupied with memories," mutters Hulk.

Ace scowls at him. It's a silent warning that makes me shiver, and I have no doubt these huge men have a nasty side. "This, Lucy, is Hulk. He's my eldest son and my Vice President. I guess that makes him your half-brother."

I raise my eyebrows. I wasn't expecting that, but now that Ace has said it, I see the similarities in their stance and build. "Oh," I mumble.

"Yeah, oh," huffs Hulk, and his standoffish behaviour makes sense.

"You called your kid Hulk?" I ask, almost smiling in amusement, hoping to break the ice.

Ace laughs. "Road names, all of us have them. You can call him by his Christian name, James, but I doubt he'll answer." It's my turn to laugh. His proper name doesn't suit him at all. For a start, he's practically a giant, standing at least six-foot-two. His muscles have muscles of their own, and I expect he works out constantly. Tattoos crawl up his exposed arms, and I decide that Hulk suits him much better because, in actual fact, he's built just like a Hulk. "I'm Max," adds Ace.

"If I had a road name, what would it be?" I ask.

The men before me exchange a look. They weren't expecting the question, but then Hulk smirks. "Lucky," he says, "because you're damn lucky to have found this guy." He pats Ace on the shoulder affectionately, and it's the first time I've seen Hulk visibly relax.

TAG

Loud cheers erupt around me as I enter the hotel room. The fight tonight was a tough one, and even though I won, it was a hard slog. My mind is elsewhere, mainly on Lucy. It's been a week since I last saw her and my heart aches. I'm craving her so badly, like an addict craves crack.

Anton approaches, slapping me hard on the back. "Well done. It was a close one tonight."

"Tell me about it."

"My father wants a word," he says, and I inwardly groan. The last thing I need is a pep talk from Conner about how I could have lost him a stupid amount of money tonight. He's sitting on a circular couch towards the back of the large room. Ella is at his side, and I scowl at the short dress she's rocking tonight. She might look amazing, but I don't want other eyes to see all that skin. Conner indicates for me to sit.

"Well done, Matteo," he drawls. "I almost broke out a sweat tonight, it was such a close one."

"It was never close, Conner. I had it in the bag. I felt like toying with my opponent." I give a cocky grin, but he doesn't fall for it. He knows I won by the skin of my teeth.

"I had a chat with Anton this evening. It appears you have a lot on your mind."

"I do?"

"My daughter?"

I pause, not sure if he's happy about this new information or not. His expression gives nothing away, and I glance at Ella, who is pressing her lips together to stop a smile escaping.

"About that—" I begin, but he cuts me off, holding his hand up to me.

"I'm not stupid, Matteo. I know you like Ella. You've been like a puppy dog around her since you got your first damn erection," he mutters. "I was waiting for the right time to raise it with you."

"Okay," I say slowly.

"The heads of each family have been invited to my home at eight this Saturday evening. I'll announce the news of your father's death followed by your engagement to Ella. It's a good match, they'll be very happy."

Ella screams excitedly and then launches herself into my arms. "Of course, you'll need to arrange the details quickly. I don't want a long engagement," adds Conner firmly. I nod, keeping Ella in my arms. My mind isn't on Ella or the wedding but the fact that I'm running out of time to kill my father and I haven't put a plan in place yet.

Ella's eyes are full of excitement, her little mind already picturing her dream wedding. She rubs her backside against my crotch, and I dig my fingers into her hip to still her. Conner stands as his right-hand man approaches. "Michael, is it sorted?" he asks, shaking his hand.

Michael nods and then they walk away together in deep discussion. This time next week, I'll be included in those kinds of discussions.

Ella wraps her arms around my neck. "Oh baby, it's really happening," she whispers. I nod, still shocked, and she places a soft kiss against my mouth. "I'm so excited to be Mrs. Ella Corallo." I repeat the name over in my head, but it doesn't sound as great since meeting Lucy. Ella pulls me to stand, leading me away from the party and into the bedroom. "I know it's a shock," she says, closing the door and clicking the lock.

"I wasn't expecting him to agree so easily," I admit.

"How could he not? Me, married to the head of the Corallo family, we're an ideal match."

"I guess." I shrug, and she runs her hands up my chest, rising onto her tiptoes to place a kiss on my lips. "We'd better get back out there," I say. I don't want her father to think I'm seducing her in this room.

"We don't have to sneak around now, we have his permission," says Ella, placing gentle kisses along my jaw line. "You've been wanting this for so long," she adds. Her hand reaches between us, and she rubs my cock through the denim jeans. I close my eyes. She's right, I've dreamed about her touching me for so long.

"You're waiting for marriage, remember," I say, gripping her wrist to halt her wandering hand.

"What's wrong?" she asks, hurt lacing her words.

"Nothing." I kiss her, hard and deep, stealing her breath. "I want it to be perfect. I want to take my time and savour you." She nods, a sulky pout on her face. "Don't sulk, baby, it'll be worth the wait."

"Now we're getting married," she says, pulling away slightly, "I don't expect to see you with any other woman."

"Of course not, my eyes are strictly on you," I promise. "And now we're getting married," I add, using her words, "I don't expect to see you in anything like this." I point to her short skirt.

Ella looks down at it and shrugs, placing her hands on her hips. "It's just a skirt."

"I don't want other men looking at you. If you're gonna be mine, I expect you to keep yourself covered. Think about it. I'd have to kill every man who disrespects me by looking at you," I say firmly. I leave the room, letting those words sink in.

Pulling out my mobile, I need to find my father, and fast.

Chapter Fifteen

LUCY

I've spent the last hour being dragged around what I now know to be called the clubhouse. It's basically a warehouse turned living space, where all the Rebellions hang out. Most of them have a room here, but a lot of the guys who have families tend to have their own place and come here to hang out and attend meetings, or church, as Ace called it. I'm enthralled by all of this. It's like a new world I knew nothing about, and I love how Ace talks about the club members. They're like one big family, and he cares about all of them.

Happy, one of the club members, hands me a drink. I'm too polite to ask what's in it, so I drink it back, wincing as the bourbon hits my throat and burns all the way down to my stomach. Happy lets out a loud cheer. "Yep, that confirms it, Pres, she's your girl." He laughs.

So far, all the guys have been lovely. They seem to accept me just on Ace's word, and I feel special, like I've always belonged here. The only person who appears offish is Hulk. "I'll introduce you to some of the old ladies," says Ace, leading me towards a group of women. They turn as I approach, and I suddenly feel self-conscious, like impressing these women is really important. "Ladies, this is Lucy. She's my daughter, Sylvia's girl."

One of the older ladies steps forward and hugs me. "I always hoped you'd come and find us," she says warmly. She's rounded and has all the signs of a mother bear, even down to her kind features. "I'm Queenie, Bear's old lady." She points across the room to a grey-haired man propping up the bar. "You need anything, you come to me." I nod.

"Me, Bear, and Queenie are some of the oldies here," explains Ace. "Been here from the beginning."

Queenie takes my hand and pulls me away from Ace. "Go, leave us to look after her," she orders, and he gives me an apologetic smile before stepping away. "This is Foxy, Trucker's old lady," says Queenie, "and this is my daughter, Piper." Piper smiles. She's more my age, and I feel at ease right away.

"Hey, lucky you. Ace is great," she says. "He's talked about his girl for years. I bet you've made his year turning up like this."

"I wasn't sure about coming, but I'm so glad I have."

Piper takes me by the hand. "Let me introduce you to some of the girls from our generation," she jokes, and her mum playfully taps her arm.

Two girls are by the bar. "Nova, Mae, this is Lucy," says Piper, and they smile. "She's the Pres' daughter."

"No fucking way," gasps Nova, "So, you're Hulk's sister?"

"Lucky cow," says Mae, sighing.

"How is it lucky? It means she can't crush on him," says Nova.

"Exactly. How nice would it be to not have to love him?" Mae groans, and we all laugh. I feel like I'm going to make some good friends here.

The next day, I go into my office with a bounce in my step. I'd spent the night thinking about my new family. I've been invited back on Saturday night for a cookout, and Piper promised it would be a brilliant night.

Keelan stands as I enter. "Thank god you're here. I tried calling you a hundred times," he says dramatically.

"Something wrong?" I ask, glancing at my watch. I'm only half an hour later than I usually am.

"Yes, a woman rang this morning to make an appointment with you, and you're cutting it close. She's due in ten minutes."

"Relax, Kee, I'm here now."

"She requested you. I tried to book her in with me, but she wasn't having any of it. She said you're the best."

I laugh. "Well, I can't argue with that."

"It sounds like a big one, though, Lucy. She talked about money being no problem."

"Great," I huff. I hate rich bitches. They expect the impossible. Like a few weeks ago, a girl from Chelsea requested twenty unicorns. She didn't know that unicorns weren't a real animal.

I pour myself a coffee and open my MacBook. "You can't afford to blow this, Lucy," says Keelan in a warning tone, and I know he's right. Last month's figures weren't great, and the last thing I need is my business failing. My mother would revel in that, and now that I've made the choice to split from Noah permanently, I have to make a good go of this.

"Relax, Kee, it'll work out, and I'll be the biggest arse licker ever, I promise."

I'm lost in my emails when the door opens, and I hear Keelan welcome the client. The voice makes me look up instantly. I'd recognise that annoying sound anywhere, and my worst fears are confirmed as Ella makes her way toward my desk. "Lucy," she says like she's happy to see me, "how wonderful to see you." Looking around, she adds, "I love this little place."

"Ella," I say, confusion on my face.

"And this is my mother, Alison." I glance at the carbon copy of Ella as her mother holds out a bony hand for me to shake, her diamond ring catching my eye.

"Ella tells me you're the best planner in London," she says.

"Thank you, maybe not the best, though," I say.

"Oh, don't be silly, of course, you are," says Ella, sitting down opposite me. Her mother does the same. "Tag highly recommends you." She arches her brow, and I wonder if Tag knows that she's here.

"So," I say, "what can I help you with?"

"I can't officially confirm the date until after Saturday," begins Ella excitedly, "but once my father has announced it, I'll call you. Anyway, I want a huge wedding, so I thought I'd book an appointment so we could make a start. The date is a minor detail." She shrugs like it's no big deal.

"And the groom didn't want to be part of the planning?" I ask casually, tapping away on my laptop. I need her to confirm it's him that she's marrying, even though deep down I know it is.

"Well, you know Tag, not one for the important things." She laughs, and the sound grates on my nerves. "But he said he'll be happy with whatever I choose, and of course, money is no object. He insists I have my dream day and just wants to make me happy. I'm thinking pink, glitter, animals, and a theme."

I knew those were the things she'd pick. All rich bitches want a tacky wedding. Tag will hate it, and so I smile, vowing to give her exactly what she wants.

"Then you'll love this," I say, opening a catalogue of previous tacky weddings I'd been forced into doing. Ella leans forward eagerly, her eyes scanning each page like she's in heaven. I catch Keelan's eye, and we share a smirk.

"Will this date be sooner rather than later?" I ask.

Ella's mother nods. "I should imagine it'll be within the next couple of weeks."

"Weeks?" I screech. "Weddings take months to plan, not weeks."

"That's why we came to you. I'm sure it'll be no problem seeing as money is no object." That's another rich person flaw, thinking everything can be done at the drop of a hat.

"I'm sorry, but we may have limited options if it's going to be weeks."

Ella pushes fake tears to her eyes, and her mother takes her hand. "Don't worry, darling, Daddy will sort this," she says soothingly. I roll my eyes. Even the Mafia can't pull off this diabolical wedding in a few weeks.

TAG

Ella pulls off her shirt, and I try not to watch as she unhooks her bra angrily. "Who the hell can't put a wedding together in a few weeks? She must be incompetent," she complains, turning on the shower. "And stop turning away from me. We're practically married."

I turn back towards her now that she's safely behind the frosted glass screen. "I was being a gentleman."

"Daddy is furious," she continues on her rant.

"Can't you just find another wedding planner?" I suggest, having no interest in all the planning.

"No, Matteo, I can't just find any planner. I want this one!"

"What's so special about this one if she can't even pull off what you want?"

"Because she fucked my fiancé, and he still thinks about her," she yells. The words penetrate my brain and then I pull open the shower door, steam billowing out. Ella's hands continue to rub soapy suds into her naked, wet body, and I try not to let that distract me.

"You went to Lucy?" I growl.

"Of course, I did. My message needs to be clear—you are mine!"

"Lucy and I are over. She knows everything."

"And yet you still think about her," she says, a dangerous glint in her eye.

"No, I don't," I lie. "I'm marrying you, aren't I?"

"But you fucked her, and now, she plays through your mind."

"Grow up, Ella. All that was for you. I did all that to get you."

"But you let her win you over. It became more than a bet and you know it. I saw the way you looked at her. I'm not blind."

"We are not having her plan our wedding!" I shout, slamming the shower door closed again. "You go against me and there will be consequences." Her laughter rings out as I leave the room.

Half an hour later, I sit in the car outside Lucy's shop. "Do you want me to go in and cancel, boss?" asks Dan, and I shake my head. It's hard seeing her again. I watch through the window as she laughs, dancing with her assistant and spinning around the room like she's the happiest person ever.

I step from the car and head over. As I push the door, she stops spinning, and when she spots me, her smile fades. "Tag."

"Hey, I came to talk about Ella."

"I told her already, you can't expect miracles with no notice. A lot of the things she wants are already booked up, but I'll do my best. Sending in the heavies won't change things."

"Heavies?" I repeat. "You think I'm here to threaten you?" I laugh, shaking my head. It's another reason we'd never work, she doesn't understand my life. "I just came to say cancel it. Ella will have to find someone else."

"Someone else? Why?"

"Well, it's a little weird, isn't it? She's done it to prove a point."

"It's not weird at all," she says indignantly. "I'm a wedding planner, and she needs one. Why is it weird?"

My eyes shift from her to her assistant. "Well, with me and you . . ." I trail off.

"There is and never was any me and you. We were a huge mistake and it was all fake. I've moved on, and you need to do the same."

"Moved on? What does that mean?"

"Just what I said. Now, if you don't mind, I have a wedding to plan. I hope you like the colour pink."

"Pink?" I repeat in disgust. "Tell me that's a joke."

She laughs. "That's what happens when you hand over your bank card and take no interest in what is supposed to be the biggest day of your life."

"Right, are you free now?"

"I'm about to go home actually," she says.

"Then bring some ideas and I'll buy you dinner."

"No. Book an appointment and bring your fiancée." She says the words bitterly, the first sign she's shown that none of this is okay with her.

"Are these the books we need?" I ask, grabbing an armful of folders and glaring at her assistant for confirmation. He nods, and I smile gratefully. "Let's go, Ten."

"No, I have plans." I don't want to know what the plans are, especially if they involve another man. I hand the files to her assistant.

"Put those in that car," I say, pointing across the street. I take Ten and effortlessly pick her up over my shoulder, slapping her arse when she screams and tries to wriggle free. Something feels right about being this close to her again, like it's where I belong.

I place her into the back seat of the car and then climb in beside her, not trusting her to jump out if I was to sit in the front. "I don't want pink or glitter or anything girly. I want class."

"Then you should have married class," she snaps, and then she slaps her hand over her mouth, realising her mistake.

"Careful, Ten, the punishment for speaking out like that could get you into trouble."

"What do you do to people who speak out?" she asks. "Same as what you do to people who don't pay up, even when they have nothing?" I glance at her. "I paid your little friend a visit, the one at the restaurant."

I'd been told that Kenny paid his debt in full just yesterday. Dan catches my eye in the mirror, and I know he's thinking the same as me. "I trust you have no issue with him now he's paid what he owes," she continues.

"And what do you know about that, Lucy?" I growl. I see her throat bob up and down as she swallows. "Because I'm hoping to God you didn't give that sleaze any money."

"What if I did?" she snaps, folding her arms across her chest defiantly.

I pinch the bridge of my nose and count to five. The car comes to a stop by Lucy's apartment. "You aren't coming in," she huffs, getting out of the vehicle.

"Dan, call Tony, then go sort Kenny. I'll deal with Miss Interfering."

"No problem, boss."

I grab the folders and follow Lucy into her building. "You have no idea what a fool Kenny is," I say as we step in the elevator. "How much did he rob from you?"

"He didn't rob it, I offered it."

"And he told you that he owed how much?"

I follow her to her apartment, and she turns to face me, her back to the door. "You aren't coming inside."

"I am."

"Leave or I'll call the police," she threatens.

"Great, say hi to Chief Graham. He wins a lot of money on my fights." Lucy stamps her foot in frustration, and I smile as we move into her apartment. "What were your plans for tonight?" I ask, placing the folders down on the kitchen counter.

"I was going on a date."

My eyes snap to hers. "With?" I ask.

"None of your business. All you need to know is he's good in bed and I'm madly in love." I know it's a lie, but it still cuts me.

"That's not funny."

"I was planning on joining Tinder tonight. I've been told it's the hottest app," she says.

"Yeah, for hook-ups," I mutter coldly.

"Exactly." I sigh. She's trying to piss me off, and it's working.

"So, how much did you give Kenny?"

"I'm not telling you."

"Because his debt was ten grand." Her face changes as she realises that Kenny is a con man and he's taken full advantage of her offer. "And now, because of you, I have to end him."

Her eyes widen. "What? No!"

"Yes. He's taken advantage of you and made a mug of me."

"He didn't ask me to pay it, I offered."

"And how much did you give him?" I yell suddenly, and she jumps in fright.

"Fifteen," she mumbles, her eyes filling with tears.

"You gave him fifteen grand? Who the hell hands over that amount to a stranger?" I yell, and her tears spill down her face. "What were you thinking?" She doesn't answer, and that pisses me off more. "This is the reason we can never work—you don't get it. Kenny is a terrible person. Us visiting weekly to collect money meant he kept his nose clean," I yell, moving into her face. "It meant he couldn't fuck kids!" Lucy gasps. "The story was so much bigger than him owing me money."

"I didn't know," she mutters.

"No, you really didn't. Ella gets me, she understands me," I shout. "You have your rose-tinted glasses on, wanting to save the world and make it pretty. Well, it isn't. None of it is!"

Lucy swipes at her tears. "I didn't know. Why are you yelling at me? If you hadn't lied in the first place, none of this would have happened. If you'd have kept me out of your stupid games!"

"I really wish I had, trust me."

"Just leave. I don't want you here."

"You don't get to call the shots, not now you've crossed over into my fucking world and meddled with shit you know nothing about."

I'm shouting again, and before I register it, she slaps me hard across the face.

"Fuck you," she hisses, backing away. I snigger, biting my lower lip as I prowl towards her. She keeps backing up until she hits the wall, and I pounce, grabbing her arms and pinning them above her head. I run my tongue over her lips, tasting salt from her tears. She inhales sharply, and I take the opportunity to deepen the kiss, pressing my erection against her stomach. She responds, kissing me back, and our mouths clash together in a hungry kiss. She hooks her leg around my thigh, and I release her hands to lift her from the floor, encouraging her to wrap her legs around my waist. I rub her breast through her shirt, and she hisses against my mouth. Fuck, I've missed this. I've missed her.

My mobile buzzes in my pocket and we freeze. It breaks the mood, and Lucy hangs her head, regretting this. I lower her back to the floor and step away to answer the call.

"Dan, all sorted?"

"Yeah, boss. There's cash in his safe. You want it back for the girl?"

"Yeah, bring it here." I disconnect the call. Lucy looks guilty as hell, and I move her hair from her face. "Dan has your money."

"I don't want it. Not if it means you've hurt Kenny."

"It's your money, you're having it back. I'll make up whatever is missing."

"I don't want your blood money. Please, Tag, just leave."

"Ten." I sigh, and she glares at me.

"Lucy. My name is fucking Lucy." She growls, covering her face with her hands. "Fuck. You're getting married, and I just let you . . ." She growls again in frustration.

"I can't control myself around you," I admit.

She grits her teeth. "Well, try. Maybe I should tell her," she adds. "Maybe she deserves to know you're a fucking dog."

"You could tell her," I say with a nod, "but it wouldn't achieve anything. She wouldn't leave me. She might just have you killed. Her father is kind of a big deal."

Lucy glares at me. "Great. So, I could be in danger?"

"Only if you open your mouth."

My phone rings again, and it's Dan announcing his arrival. I go to Lucy's intercom and press the unlock button. I wait for him at her door, and when he appears, there are splatters of blood on his white shirt. I hand him my jacket, and he puts it on before handing me an envelope stuffed with cash. "Five grand," he confirms.

I take it in to Lucy, who's sitting by the window staring out with a blank expression. I hate that I can't stay away, and I hate seeing her like this, knowing it's all my fault. "It's not the full amount," I say, placing it on the table. It brings her out of her daydream and she stares at the envelope.

"I don't want it."

"It's your money, Lucy. Jesus, you're so fucking stubborn. Take your damn money and I'll get the rest to you. And I'll get Ella to find another wedding planner. I'm sorry she came to you."

"Whatever you want, Tag." Her voice is cold and distant.

"I can't have what I want," I mutter, and she glances at me. "Take care, Ten."

Chapter Sixteen

♥

LUCY

Saturday rolls around quickly. I'm excited as I drive into the car park of The Rebellion MC. There are bikes parked up all along one side, and I spot Ace standing outside having a cigarette. He smiles wide as I approach and he embraces me, "I'm so pleased you've come back. I was worried we'd scared you off."

"I've been looking forward to seeing you all again," I confess.

"But mainly me." Scar grins, stepping outside to join us.

"Of course," I agree, laughing. Scar is definitely the joker of the bunch.

"I had a call earlier from your friend," says Ace, dropping his cigarette and crushing it under his heavy boot. "Tag."

"You did?" I ask, trying not to sound too interested. "Although, he's not my friend."

"He was checking to see if you'd been in touch."

"What did you tell him?"

"I didn't tell him anything. I don't know him well enough yet."

"Yet?" I ask.

"Well, if he's a friend of yours . . ." He trails off and nods towards the gates as they open. "Speak of the devil."

I whip my head around, watching in horror as Tag's car parks and he steps out. He places his shades over his eyes and then strolls towards us. He looks hot in his denim jeans and black T-shirt. "Again, he's not my friend," I hiss at Ace. He doesn't have time to react before Tag is next to me, smiling. He shakes hands with Ace first and then Scar. "Thanks so much for the invite," he says.

"No problem. Thanks for putting this one in touch with me."

Tag smiles at me. "I thought you needed to know what a wonderful daughter you have." He's too smooth, and I roll my eyes.

"Scar will show you inside. Get yourself a drink and we'll be in shortly," says Ace. He waits until Scar and Tag are gone before turning back to me. "What do you mean he isn't your friend?"

"It's complicated," I mutter. "We were friends, but things happened and now we don't really see eye to eye. In fact, I don't know why he came today."

"Darlin', if the President of the Rebellions invites you to a cookout, you show up," says Ace, confidentiality.

"Did he know I'd be here?"

"No," he says. "I told you, he called to ask for a meet. He needs something from me, and I think he was waiting to see if I'd mention you, which I didn't. I wanted to see him face to face. Besides, he ain't so bad if he got us together again after all these years."

"You don't know him like I do," I warn as we head inside.

"They'll all be out back," says Ace, leading me out another door and into a large field. There are far more people than when I came the other night. Kids are running around laughing and playing, adults are sitting on blankets, some enjoying the rare sunshine and others chatting happily to one another. "Go and mingle," he encourages.

I head straight for Piper and her friends. They made me feel welcome before, and as I approach, they stand and embrace me. "We're so happy you came back," says Piper.

"That's what Ace said." I laugh. "He was worried I'd been scared off."

"We're a lively bunch. It takes a while to get used to us."

"I couldn't wait to come back."

"We were just wondering if the hot boxer was with you?" asks Nova. I glance over my shoulder to see Tag chatting to a few of the bikers.

"Not really. Ace invited him thinking we're friends."

"And you're not?" Piper questions.

I shrug, lowering myself onto their blanket. "We were. He used me."

"I'd let him use me," says Mae, sighing dreamily, and I laugh.

"He's getting married."

"So, how come he used you? What happened?" Piper asks.

I give them a quick rundown, and they all stare open-mouthed. "What a dick," hisses Piper, and I nod in agreement. "Does Ace know this?"

"No. I'm so over the whole thing. I'm just gonna ignore him."

A female comes running across the field from the clubhouse, yelling and screaming. We all turn to stare. "Oh god, that's Foxy," whispers Piper. "She's crazy when it comes to Trucker."

I watch in astonishment as she dives towards Trucker, hitting him hard across the face and yelling about another woman. The way he towers over her scares the crap out of me, but Foxy doesn't back down. "Wow, she isn't even a bit scared," I whisper back. "He terrifies me."

"These guys might look the part, but they'd rather die than hurt a woman. Trucker loves the bones of the crazy bitch."

I watch as he grips her arms and holds them by her side, then he places a light kiss on her mouth, and she stops yelling. "I love you," he says firmly, and she almost melts against him. He picks her up in his arms and carries her back towards the clubhouse.

"Where's he taking her?" I ask.

"To fuck her brains out probably," says Mae. "That's their thing—they fight and fuck. It's a vicious circle."

"Wow. Are all the guys like that?"

"Some," mutters Nova. "Most of the guys are mad about their women. There're a few single brothers who haven't found that yet, like your brother."

"I can see why. He's scary too."

Piper laughs. "You just have to know how to handle him."

"And you know all the ways in which to handle him," says Mae, grinning. Piper blushes and throws a handful of grass at her.

"You and Hulk?" I ask, surprised.

"No, he won't commit to her," says Nova. "He should be snapping her up cos he won't find anyone better."

Piper sighs. "Be quiet."

"Oh, he's coming over," hisses Mae, and we all glance up to see Hulk heading our way. Piper blushes a deeper red, and I want to laugh.

"You came," he grates out, and I nod. "And you brought Mafia into our home?"

"No," I snap, "Ace invited him. I didn't know he was coming."

"Piper, come," he snaps.

"No," she says coldly, and he glowers at her. "I'm with my friends."

"We need to talk."

"You could have come and talked to me anytime. Instead, I find you doing a whole lot more than talking with Kat." My eyes dart back and forth between the two. It's hard to see whether they have something special because Piper is clearly upset with him.

"I'm not asking you, Pip, I'm telling you. Get the fuck up and come with me." His voice gets higher with each word, but Piper stays put. "You're defying an order from the VP?" he adds.

She shrugs. "Seems that way."

"I'm gonna throw you over my shoulder," he warns.

"And I'll call for Queenie." This seems to halt him from taking Piper against her will. He turns to see where Queenie is, which isn't far, then he lets out a growl.

"Please, baby, just come and talk to me." The change in his tone seems to get around Piper's stubbornness, and she sighs before pushing to her feet.

"If I'm not back in five minutes, send Queenie in to find me," she throws over her shoulder before pushing past Hulk and heading inside. I love how sassy these women seem to be, not letting these huge men push them around. I could learn a lot here.

TAG

I finally pluck up the courage to approach Lucy. I've never been scared of anything in my life, but right now, I'm petrified of how she will react to me. We keep being pushed together. When I called Ace, I was trying to figure out if Lucy had contacted him, but he was closed off, guarded. I didn't want to mention her in case she'd decided not to bother. But Ace might be the solution to my other little problem.

I check my watch again, finding I have a few hours before I have to end my father. Seeing Lucy here today was a surprise, but I'm happy for her. Ace is a good man, and I know he'll take care of her. "You're marrying Conner Martinez's daughter?" asks Scar, adding an uncertain laugh.

"Yeah, in a few weeks." I check my watch again, my nerves kicking in.

"She's hot, but she has a rep," he says, and my ears prick up.

"A rep?" I repeat.

"Yeah. Surely you know, everyone does."

I feel my defences coming up and my stance changes. He picks up on it and backs off. "Man, I didn't mean any harm. You ask anyone, she has a bad rep. I assumed you knew." He pulls out his phone and spends a second flicking through it. "Look." He holds it to me, and I blink to make sure I'm seeing right. There's a photograph of Ella in a sexy pose, her legs spread wide and a scrap of material covering just enough to hide her pussy. Her hands cover her naked breasts.

"Where did you get this?" I growl.

"She posted it on her social media," he says, pressing another button and bringing up Ella's profile. Her username is Sexy Mafia Princess. I take his phone and begin to scroll through. Photo after photo is her practically naked.

"So, these are just a bunch of photographs, what did you mean about her bad rep?"

"She comes around the biker bars a lot, yah know, looking for . . . a bit of rough."

I scoff. "That's impossible. She's never without her minder."

"The gay one?" asks Scar. "Yeah, he's always there."

I curl my fists in anger. "So, you're telling me she sleeps around?"

Scar nods. "Yeah. That's why I was so surprised when you said you were marrying her, a man of your stature. Rumour has it you're stepping into your father's shoes."

I pull out my phone and find Ella on my Instagram. I screenshot some of her pictures and forward them on to Anton. He'll hit the roof and so will Conner. It instantly buzzes to life and I answer. "What the fuck are you sending me those for?" yells Anton.

"What the fuck is your sister doing putting those on social media?"

"What?"

"There's a whole bunch of them under the name Sexy Mafia Princess. I'm hearing all kinds of shit about her, Anton. Find her. I'll be over soon."

"She's out with her minder. I'll call him and get him to bring her to the house."

"Actually, don't. I know where she might be. I'll bring her."

I disconnect the call and smile at Scar. "You fancy taking me around some bars?"

"Yeah, sure, I'll clear it with the Pres." He goes off to discuss it with Ace, and I go over to where Lucy sits. She looks happy and relaxed, sipping on a glass of gin.

"Are you ignoring me?" I ask.

"Yes, you're blocking my sun."

"I didn't know you'd be here. I came to see your father because I need his help with something."

"Funny that you keep turning up where I am. And you hardly know him. Why are you suddenly so desperate for his help?"

"Hey, I didn't say desperate," I correct her, "but I figured if you'd been in touch, he owed me."

"You owed me after your disgusting behaviour."

"Maybe this is fate," I suggest, smirking.

"I doubt that very much. Have you set a date for the wedding?" She arches a brow.

"There might not be one, Ten." I wink and head off. I have business to attend to.

We spend the next hour driving around different biker bars that Scar points me in the direction of. So far, Ella hasn't been in any of them. "Let's try this last one. If she isn't in here, I'll get Dan on it."

Inside, it's dull and half empty. A woman is smoking a cigarette behind the bar, and as we enter, she smiles. "What can I get you boys?"

I hold up my mobile phone with a picture of Ella showing. "Seen her?"

"Yeah, she's out back. Please take her home, she's wasted and it's bad for business."

The door from the toilets opens and Ella's minder almost drops to the floor in shock. "Don't fucking move," I growl. He stands still as I move past him to the back door. "Make sure he stays there," I tell Scar.

The door opens into an alleyway. It's getting dark and I can just about make out the industrial-sized waste bins. I move past them and spot Ella. She has her back against the wall and her hands tangled in the hair of a guy who has his face buried between her legs. I lean back against the opposite wall. I can't deny that I'm pissed and hurt. She was supposed to be saving herself for marriage. I almost laugh to myself, thinking of all those times I've restrained myself.

Ella begins to quiver, her legs shaking. The guy stands and positions himself between her legs. I wince as he lunges forwards, causing Ella to scream out. Even if she was before, she certainly ain't a virgin now.

I step out of the shadows. Ella's eyes are closed in pleasure, and they don't spring open until I have my knife against the guy's throat. She screams when her eyes connect with mine. I feel wild, the thirst for blood edging me on as I pull the blade across the guy's skin. He gurgles, coughing and spluttering before his hand reaches to his throat, trying to cover the spurting wound. Ella is splashed in his blood as it coats her bare breasts and soaks into the top she has pulled down around her waist.

"The wedding's off," I say coldly. The guy drops to the ground, and I grab Ella by the arm. Tugging her, she trips over his body, falling against me.

"Tag, please, it wasn't like that. I just—"

"I don't wanna hear it, Ella. Fucking some nobody in an alleyway? I can't marry you now!" I glare at her in disgust. I pull out my mobile and type out the address to Tony, using the code for clean-up. He'll take care of it.

I drag Ella through the bar as she tries to tug up her top. "I'll take care of the mess out back," I say to the bar owner. I chuck a roll of cash onto the bar, and she snatches it up quick, nodding. She's used to this with it being a biker bar, so she won't say a word to anyone. "Don't let anyone out there until my guys get here."

Scar follows me to the car, dragging Ella's minder along behind. I chuck the car keys to Scar and get into the back with Ella. Her fake tears are pissing me off and I turn away from her. "I'm sorry, Tag. I just get so sick of being the perfect daughter. Sometimes I need to let loose."

"In every sense of the word," I mutter.

"And I'd like it to be known that I've tried to talk sense into her," says her minder.

"Tell it to Conner," I snap.

"Tag, you know what she's like. I was under her orders."

"You liar," screeches Ella. "You've never tried to stop me."

"Enough," I yell. "You can both explain yourself to Conner. I'm simply delivering you." Ella cries harder, and I role my eyes in annoyance. She could win awards for her acting.

I direct Scar to Conner's large home, where Conner and Anton are waiting on the steps. As we come to a stop, Anton rips open the car door and drags Ella from it. She lands on her knees, and he pulls her to stand by her hair. I wince, knowing they won't be kind. She's effectively shamed their family, but I still detest the violence.

Climbing out the car, I open the passenger front door and indicate for her minder to also step out. He's barely stood up when a loud bang rings out. I duck out of instinct and then step back as the minder's body falls to the ground. There's a perfect circle between his eyes where the bullet entered his head, and as he lays on the ground lifeless, his eyes open but unseeing, a pool of crimson fluid spreads over the white stones beneath him.

Ella's screams ring out. Violence isn't usually displayed in front of the women, yet this is the second time this evening that she's witnessed it. Conner grips her upper arm and marches her over to the body of her minder, forcing her to look down at him. "This is on you," he seethes. "His blood is on your hands."

"I'm sorry," she cries desperately.

Conner holds his mobile to her face, displaying her social media pictures. "Look at this shit. You look like a whore," he spits. "You want other men looking at you?" She looks away, having the decency to appear embarrassed.

"No," she whispers.

"Matteo doesn't want you now, you repulse him. I'm sending you away to live with your grandmother in Scotland." I watch as he drags her into the house, slamming the door closed behind them.

"Brother." Anton sighs, slapping my shoulder.

"When did she get so rebellious, Ant, and why didn't we see it?"

"Maybe we were too busy playing games, Tag. We lost sight of what was important to us."

Scar steps from the car. He looks uncomfortable, and I regret dragging him along to my domestic problems. It's embarrassing. "Wedding is off then? Man, I feel bad. I should never have opened my mouth."

"You did us all a favour. We had no clue she was behaving that way. Conner will see it as the ultimate disrespect. She'll have to move away now, until she can prove she's learned her lesson," I say. "I owe you one, man."

We drive back to the Rebellion clubhouse. My mind is full of questions, like why don't I feel too hurt about Ella but instead feel relieved?

"I have to say, Tag, you don't seem too cut up about Ella," Scar says.

"The thing is, when I was pursuing my dream to marry Ella, I fell for someone else."

"Lucy?" He smirks, glancing over at me.

I smile. Even her name brightens my day. "How'd yah guess?"

"She's a stunner. The fact that you went to the trouble of finding Ace for her says a lot."

"Yeah. Trouble is, she doesn't understand my world. She's an innocent."

"And you're scared of corrupting her?"

"I'm scarred she'll accept it too easily and it'll change her in ways that might ruin her."

"Funny you should say that. I had the exact same conversation with Ace after she'd turned up. But yah know what I said to him? It's not up to you, or him—it's Lucy's choice. Be honest so she goes in with her eyes wide open. She might surprise you with how tough she really is."

Scar's words make sense. If I'm honest and she walks away, then at least I've given her the option. If I walk away and don't even give her a chance, I'll never know. I can't live never knowing.

Chapter Seventeen

♥

LUCY

I'm drunk and it feels nice. I'm more relaxed than I've been in months. "I need your keys," says Ace, holding out his hand expectantly. "For your apartment," he clarifies.

"Why?" I ask.

"I'm packing up Noah's shit and sending it to him. After what he's done, I don't want him anywhere near you." Hulk stands by his side, his face stern, and I decide not to argue and hand my keys over. I'd told the girls all about my relationship with Noah and how it ended. Queenie made it her mission to tell Ace, and for once, it's nice to have people care for me.

"I have some other business to take care of, so we'll be an hour or two," he adds. I feel privileged that he's bothering to explain to me why he'll be gone for some time.

Mae swoons. "Wow, how cute is that? I've always wondered what kind of father Ace would be to a daughter, and he's exactly as I imagined."

"You have serious daddy issues, swooning over the Pres like that," says Nova, laughing, and Mae nods, clearly in full agreement.

I've discovered that Piper, Nova, and Mae have grown up in the MC. Piper's father, Bear, is one of the founding members, along with Ace. Nova's father is the club's doctor. I've yet to meet Doc, but I hear he's also big on family. Mae's father was killed by a rival MC years ago, leaving her and her mother with the club. Her mother, Bernie, cooks for the guys, and they adore her.

"I need to bring Tyra and Bel here. You'll love them," I say. I feel like they'll all get along well, and now that I've stepped away from Penelope and the clique, I'll have more time for my real friends.

"Looks like your man is back," says Piper, nudging against my arm. I look over in the direction of her stare, and sure enough, Tag is by the bar with Scar. I can't help the warm, fuzzy feeling I get inside when I see him. I sigh, and the girls giggle. "That's pure love in your eyes."

"It is not," I protest. "He's an arse. It'd never work. He's part of something bigger, and I can't handle that."

"Of course, you can. You're Ace's daughter, you can handle anything," says Piper, and I laugh. If only that was true. She takes my hand and pulls me to stand. "We need to dance," she cries, wiggling her hips to a song that begins to pump from the speakers. "Turn it up, Whiskey," she yells to the bartender. He shakes his head and laughs, turning up the song.

The other girls whoop and holler, joining us. There's a space between the tables where we can dance and I let the girls pull me around as we laugh and wave our arms around. It feels good. As I spin, I hit against a hard body. Tag's face looks unimpressed as he glowers down at me, and my smile fades. I don't want another fight.

"I need to talk to you," he says. Previous experience tells me I shouldn't argue because he always gets his way in the end. I follow him outside, and when the fresh air hits me, I suddenly feel dizzy. "Ace tells me he's giving Noah a message tonight. You aren't getting back together?"

I shake my head and lean myself against the wall to keep my balance. "How's the wedding plans coming along?"

"They aren't," he says dryly. "Ella is moving to Scotland as we speak."

"Oh," I mutter, "but I thought—"

"It's over. She's betrayed me, and she's damn lucky her father is Conner Martinez because I don't know what I'd do if . . ." He stops talking and shakes his head.

"You're hurt," I observe, and his eyes fix to mine.

"Not over Ella," he says. "Hurt that I've been an idiot."

"It's never nice to realise you've been made a fool of," I say, raising an accusing brow.

Tag nods, smiling. "Maybe this is payback for how I treated you."

We fall silent before my curiosity gets the better of me. "What did she do to betray you?"

"It's not important. But we're both single now."

I laugh. "I guess so."

"Which means we have nothing standing in our way."

"Oh god, please don't hit on me, Tag," I groan. "Not after everything that's happened between us." He steps closer. I feel trapped against the wall, and I turn my head so he can't lay any surprise kisses on me.

"Why are you denying what I know you want," he growls close to my ear.

"It's too late for us, Tag. What you did was unforgivable. I was a bet . . . a fucking bet. And now your prize has betrayed you, you want to hit me up again? No, thanks." I shove past him and go back inside, feeling strong and empowered while my inner girl is sobbing in the corner and squeezing my heart.

TAG

I watch the sway of Lucy's arse as she goes back inside the clubhouse. It must have felt good for her to blow me off like that, and I expected it. She isn't going to forgive me easily, but it doesn't mean I'm ready to give up.

My phone beeps and a photograph of my father laying still and covered in blood stares at me. I text Ace back.

Me: Video it. Conner won't believe a picture.

He calls, and I answer straight away. "What if he notices him breathing or something?" he snaps. "I'm not a fucking miracle worker."

"Get him to hold his breath," I suggest. "His life depends on good acting."

"Right, I'm on it. Are you still at the club? Is Lucy okay?"

"Yeah, she's fine. I was just chatting to her actually."

"After tonight, you owe me, brother. Remember that."

I sigh and disconnect the call. Owing the Rebellions might come back to bite me in the arse. I couldn't use anyone who could go back to Conner and tell him the truth, that my father isn't dead and he'll be on the first plane out of here after the video of his fake death is done. I needed someone not connected to the Mafia, and the MC is completely separate, refusing to have any business with us.

I wait another five minutes before I receive the video. It's convincing, so I call Dan to collect me, and we make our way back to Conner's. It's almost nine, so I'm an hour late, but he'll let it go after everything with Ella.

I find Conner with the other men in his meeting room. Everyone looks very official in their suits while I'm still in my jeans and black T-shirt. Conner shakes my hand and leans in close. "I'm sorry about everything with Ella, son. I'm deeply ashamed."

"It's done. Is she gone?"

"No, first thing tomorrow." I nod, producing my mobile. I hold it up for him to see the video, and he smiles, patting me on the back.

I move around the room, greeting the other men. Anton thrusts a whiskey into my hand, and I drink it down, coughing as it burns. I hold out the empty glass so he can top it up.

"Gentlemen, may I have your attention," Conner says firmly and then waits for the chatter to die down. "I think you all know why we are here. Matteo, join me," he orders, holding his arm open. I step next to him, and he places it around my shoulder. "It's done. As agreed, Matteo will now step into his father's shoes as head of the Corallo family."

There are a few cheers and then I'm swamped with back slaps and handshakes. I feel honoured and proud. The only thing that would make this better would be to have Lucy by my side.

The men raise a glass to me, and I drink down the amber liquid, letting it be refilled again. "And now, for the women," announces Conner.

The door opens and scantily-clad women enter. They smile and make themselves busy, chatting to the men. A leggy blonde wraps her hand around my arm and smiles. "Tag," she whispers, "come with me."

I pull free because the last complication I need is another woman. I turn to Anton, who is chatting happily to one of the girls. "I'm going to see Ella," I say, and he waves me away, not showing any interest.

Taking the stairs two at a time, I tap lightly on Ella's door. When she doesn't answer, I pop my head in. She turns a tear-streaked face in my direction, and when she sees it's me, she lays back down, pressing her cheek into her pillow.

"Did he hurt you?" I ask.

"Like you care," she sniffles.

"I do care, El, you know I do. What the fuck happened? Why did you do all that shit?"

"You wouldn't believe me even if I told you."

"I would, so talk to me."

"Since I was seven," she sniffs, pushing herself to sit, "my father has been coming into my room at night." I freeze, my breath stuck in my throat. "It started as a cuddle, and I liked that he cuddled me." Ella begins to cry. "No one would believe me."

"Jesus, El, are you being serious?"

"See, you don't believe me," she yells. "He began touching me, telling me it was our little secret and that no one could know. You were supposed to get me out of this hell."

I growl. "Are you saying what I think you're saying?"

"Conner Martinez has been forcing himself on me for years, and now, he's sending me away because I disgust him. I DISGUST HIM!" She screams the last part.

My heart hammers in my chest. Conner's been like a second father to me. He's a man of power and great respect. It doesn't seem real. I pull Ella into my arms, and she sobs against my shoulder. "I hate him," she cries.

"At least if you're in Scotland, you're away from him."

"He'll visit, you know he will. I'm never going to get away from him now. You know why he's delayed me going to Scotland? So he can spend one last night with me." She looks up, staring past me. "Anton," she whispers, and I spin to see the pale face of her brother glaring at us.

"Anton," I say warily, standing. He doesn't take his eyes from his sister, and I realise he's heard our conversation. He suddenly turns and leaves the room, slamming the door hard behind him. Ella scrambles from the bed, shoving me out of the way and yelling Anton's name over and over. I run after her as she rushes down the stairs, trying to catch up with Anton's long strides. As I reach the office door, a loud bang rings out and I pull Ella from the room, pushing her to the floor and drawing my gun. I point it towards the door. "Stay down," I whisper to her, and I rise to my feet.

Anton is holding his gun to the ceiling, a large hole above his head. "Is it true?" he asks, glaring at his father.

"What the fuck is going on, Anton?" yells Conner, his face furious. Another of the men goes to reach for his gun, and I shake my head, warning him not to get involved.

"Have you been fucking your daughter, my sister?" Anton screams, shaking the gun and pointing it at Conner.

"What shit is she spouting now? Is she so desperate to get out of going to Scotland?" asks Conner, adding a nervous laugh.

"I'm not lying." I turn towards Ella's shaky voice. "Every night, since I was seven." She then holds up her cell phone and Conner's voice fills the room.

"You stupid slut! Wasn't I giving it to you enough? You've always been a greedy little cunt." Conner pales. *"Don't think by going to Scotland you'll be safe. You belong to me, and even if Tag took your sorry arse back, I'd still be paying you visits."*

Everyone turns to Conner. "She asked for it. She's a dirty slut," he growls.

Another loud shot rings out, and we all duck as Conner falls to the ground, blood spilling onto the fluffy cream carpet. Anton pulls Ella into his arms, and she sobs into his chest. "I'm so sorry, El. So, so sorry," he repeats, kissing her hair.

Maxim, the head of the Snow family, steps forward. He shakes Anton's hand, bowing his head slightly. I don't know the logistics of this situation, but I'm guessing Anton will step into his father's shoes, and as the other men step forward and kiss Anton's hand, their heads bowed, I realise that I'm right. I also step forward, kissing his hand and lowering my head as a sign of respect.

Anton leans down and pulls the family ring from his father's hand. He spits on him. "Michael," he calls, and Conner's right hand man steps inside the room, his eyes darting around at the chaos before him. "Get rid of this mess," Anton orders.

"Yes, sir," he says, ever the professional.

Chapter Eighteen

LUCY

I brush my teeth to try and get rid of the vomit taste in my mouth. *Why did I drink so much?* There's a loud banging on my door, and I look at my watch. It's almost five in the morning. I prepare myself for the wrath of Noah, who I doubt will go quietly just because Ace has told him to. I pull on a shirt to cover my nakedness as the banging continues. "Alright, I'm coming," I yell.

I rip the door open and am pushed back inside. "I know you hate me, but I need you right now," pants Tag, his hands roaming under my shirt.

"What the hell?" I growl, shoving him away. He tugs at his hair. His eyes are wild and his breathing is deep and fast.

"Sorry, I . . . I just . . ." He trails off and then growls, tugging at his hair again in frustration.

I sense the desperation in his tone and take his hand. I lead him to my couch and push him to sit down. "Take a breath and start from the beginning."

For the first time, I note that Tag looks vulnerable and scared. "The last few hours have been crazy. I need to feel normal, like myself."

"You're not making any sense Tag."

"Matteo," he growls. "Call me Matteo." I notice he's shaking and there's blood splatters on his jeans. He sees me looking at them and then rubs at them like it'll make them disappear. "I don't want you to see this, see me like this, but every so often, it gets too much, and that's when I realise I don't have anyone. Not really."

"What about Ella or Anton?" His expression looks pained, and he rubs his face hard.

"Ella. Poor fucking Ella," he groans. "I can't get her out of my mind."

"What happened between you?"

"I told you, she betrayed me," he says coldly. "I just need you, please, Luce." He's almost begging, and my heart breaks for him.

"What do you need from me?" I ask, and he stands, taking my hand. He tugs me towards my bedroom.

"Just to lay with you. Nothing else, I promise."

I nod. "Okay," I relent. "Okay."

I pull the covers back and climb into the cool sheets. Tag follows, laying on his side and pulling me into his arms. He buries his nose into my hair and breathes me in. "Be careful, I smell of vomit," I whisper.

"You smell of vanilla. Are you sick?" he mumbles into my hair.

"No, I drank way too much."

"That can't happen when you're mine," he whispers, pulling me tighter against him.

"Tag," I say, my tone warning.

"Matteo. Call me Matteo." We fall silent, and within minutes, I hear Tag's breathing deepen and light snores fill the room.

A few hours later, I hear movement and open one eye. Tag is creeping from the room. I sit up, and he freezes, turning slowly to face me. "You going somewhere?" I ask with a smile.

Tag's eyes dart from me to the door and then back to me. "Erm," he pauses, looking unsure, "I didn't mean to wake you."

"It's fine."

"I thought it'd be best if I just leave, save any awkward conversations," he says, adding a wince.

"So, you were sneaking out of here?" I laugh again, but I feel insulted. He came to me in his hour of need, and now, he's leaving with no explanation.

Tag sighs. The haunted look has left his eyes, and he stares at me blankly. "I shouldn't have turned up like that. It wasn't fair to you. I should go," he says, pointing to the door and edging closer to it.

"You came to me and now you're acting like I'm a stalker. If you want to leave, Tag, you don't have to sneak out. I won't beg you to stay."

"I've offended you . . . again. I keep fucking up." He sighs again and rubs his forehead. "It would never work between us."

"Christ, Tag, I haven't asked for a relationship," I almost screech. "You came to me."

"I know. I'm just saying, it wouldn't work."

"Who are you trying to convince, me or yourself?" I snap.

"Both of us. I'm relying on you to be the adult, so every time I turn up here—and there will be many times that I do—you need to send me away." He moves back to the bed and sits on the edge, taking my hand and giving me a serious look. "You're too good for me, Lucy, way too good. I'll ruin you, corrupt you, shock you, scare you. All those things you thought of when you discovered who I really was, they're all true. I *am* that person. I don't want to taint your beauty with all the bad that's in me." He brushes his hand against my cheek, and I turn my face into his touch. "I'm trying to do the right thing, be the good guy."

"I'm honoured." I smile.

Tag leans in towards me, placing a gentle kiss against my cheek. Instinct takes over, and although my head screams no, my heart does a happy dance as I turn my mouth to his and we clash together. Hunger takes over, controlling us as we pull at each other's clothes while our tongues taste each other. I grip his hair, leaning back until I'm laying down and Tag is on top of me. He pushes my shirt up and groans. "You've been panty-less all night, right next to me?" I grin, nodding.

His mouth crashes against mine again, and I feel him reach between us, lining his cock with my entrance. As he enters me, I cry out, digging my nails into his back. The friction from his swollen erection is too much to take, and I begin to see stars the minute he moves. I don't care that it shows my desperation for him as the orgasm quickly rips through me. "You were supposed to be the responsible one," he groans, thrusting hard and pushing me up the bed.

"I never promised," I pant.

"I don't know how I'm going to let you go, Ten," he admits, burying his nose into my hair and breathing me in. "You're my new drug." I want to tell him to get his fix from me every time, but I keep my mouth closed, shutting my eyes tight and focusing on the amazing things he's doing to my body.

Tag pulls out of me, tapping my arse so that I turn onto my front. He climbs over me, his legs either side of my thighs, and then he pushes his erection back into me. It feels tighter this way, fuller. Tag takes a handful of my hair, tugging gently so that my head is turned to the side and I'm looking at him. "Keep your eyes on me, Ten," he growls. There's something sexy about staring into the eyes of such a mysterious, dangerous man while he fucks you hard.

My fingers grip the sheets beneath me, bunching them into my fists as Tag slams into me. His eyes darken and his pupils dilate, and then he growls. It's feral and completely hot, and as he shudders his release into me, I cry out as another orgasm rolls through my body. This time, it's slow and never-ending, rippling through me, and when it finally begins to ebb away, I collapse face down onto the bed.

"That was hot," he pants, slapping my backside as he pulls from me. He climbs from the bed and goes into the bathroom, and I hear the shower running. I have no energy to follow him, and I doubt my legs are up to supporting me just yet, so I wrap the sheets around me and stay in bed.

TAG

I laid awake for an hour before Lucy woke earlier this morning. I watched her sleeping and tried to think of different ways in which I could keep her in my life. I came up with none. My only option would be to keep doing this, turning up unannounced, fuck, and then leave. She deserves more than that, but a relationship couldn't work. She'd never understand the lifestyle. She'd ask endless questions that I wouldn't be able to answer, not without implicating her into things. The shit I've done, the things I'll be expected to do, will fuck me up, just like yesterday did, and eventually, I'll become like my father, cold and distant. I'll make stupid mistakes and break Lucy's heart. I'm saving her by walking away.

I step out of her shower and dry off quickly. I didn't use a condom, but I haven't mentioned it to her. The chances are that one time won't hurt, and I guess a part of me hopes that if I've put a baby in her belly, I'll have no choice but to make her mine. I go into the bedroom and begin to dress. Lucy is asleep again, laying on her stomach, wrapped in her bed sheets with her face towards the window. She looks innocent and beautiful like this, and I commit her picture to memory.

Pushing my feet into my shoes, I grab my jacket from the chair in the corner of her bedroom. With one last look, I step out of the room. I have to walk away now. I can't do this again.

Outside, I check my phone. I have two missed calls from Anton, another from Ella, and one from Ace. I call Ace first. "Brother," he says. "Did Conner buy it?" It's not common knowledge yet about Conner, but I decide that Ace should know, so I tell him that Conner is no longer with us and that Anton is now in charge. I don't go into details, as that shit is strictly family business.

"Shit, man, sorry to hear that. Look, gather yourself and then come and see me. With Conner gone, there might be room to rediscuss our alliance with each other." I'm surprised by this—the MC has never wanted to move with the Mafia. I agree to speak with Anton and then call in to see him at the club.

Next, I call Anton. "Man, where the hell are you? Tony didn't even know where to find you."

"Sorry." I sigh. "Things got crazy last night, didn't they? I just needed to shut off for a few hours."

"Understandable. Come over, we need to talk."

When I get to Anton's family home, he's in the office. It's odd seeing him behind the desk instead of Conner. "Suits you," I say with a smirk.

He groans. "Fuck, man, what the fuck was that last night?"

I sit down opposite him. "Fucked up shit." I sigh. "Is Ella okay?"

"I think so. She cried, a lot, and spent time talking to my mum, who's heartbroken. How did none of us see it, Tag?"

I shake my head. I'd been asking myself the same question. "I just thought they were close," I reply with a shrug.

"Me too. Knowing what he did . . ." Anton shudders. "At least the fucker can't do it again."

"So, now we're both bosses," I say, grinning. "I feel like we should celebrate. We always wondered what it would be like to be here." As kids, we'd talked about how we'd run the organisation.

"Now we're here, it feels a little premature, like I'm not ready for it."

"Anton, you'll do great. You were born for this role."

There's a knock on the door and Ella enters. She has no makeup on and her eyes are red and puffy from the tears she's shed. I stand, and she throws herself into my arms. "Thank you for believing me."

I sigh. "I can't believe you'd ever think that I wouldn't, El."

Anton heads for the door. "You two catch up. I'll go and see how Mum's doing."

He closes the door behind him, and Ella steps back from me. "I was convinced no one would ever believe me over him. He told me everyone would turn against me."

"He was wrong."

"Is there still a chance?" she mumbles, twisting her fingers together like she's nervous.

"For us?" I ask. I don't want to break her heart any more than it's already broken, but I have to be honest for us both. I shake my head. "Ella, I love you, I really do, but I don't think I'm in love with you. I thought I was, but as time's gone on, I've realised that I don't feel that way about you."

Ella nods, her eyes full of sadness. "I get it. I wouldn't want me either, used goods and all." She shrugs and then adds a smile to lighten the tone.

"Baby, it's got nothing to do with any of that. I have feelings for someone else. It wasn't intentional, it just happened. And although I can never be with her, it would be unfair for me to be with you."

"You fell for the party planner?" she mutters, and I nod. It feels good to admit it. "You're a fool if you're telling yourself you can't be with her because of who you are. My mother wasn't born into this, and she stuck by my father. Your mother did the same."

"And I saw first-hand what it's done to both of them. I won't turn her into something she's not."

Ella kisses me on the cheek. "You're a good man, Tag. If she makes you happy, then you should go for it."

I take Anton with me to see Ace, it makes sense now that he's in charge, and we're welcomed into the clubhouse by Scar. There's something about this guy that I like. He leads us to Ace's office. The door is open wide, and Ace is leaning back in his chair with his heavy boots resting on his desk. "Come in, boys," he grins, "take a seat."

I relax back, feeling good vibes, and for the first time since Anton put that bullet in Conner, I'm hopeful.

Chapter Nineteen

Six months later...

LUCY

The banging on my door startles me. Checking the time, I see that it's almost eleven in the morning. I was so tired that I slept right through from the second my head hit the pillow at midnight. I pulled off a huge wedding yesterday for one of my mother's friends. Even though the bride is my mother's age, she married a man half that. It was a great day, and everything ran smooth for a change. I even managed to make my mother smile a few times. She almost admitted that I'd done a great job.

I pull my hair up into a tie as I make my way to the front door. Pulling it open, I find Hulk standing before me with his usual annoyed expression. "Stranger," he grits out, stepping through the doorway and accidentally pushing me out of the way with his huge body.

"Please, come in," I huff sarcastically.

"What you've done to Ace is shit," he snaps, turning on me the minute I enter the kitchen.

"What did I do?"

"Showing up and making Ace think you were back and then going silent on him."

I fold my arms across my chest defensively. "I haven't gone silent on him," I argue, but even as the words fall from my lips, I know I'm lying.

I'd seen Ace a few more times after everything that happened between me and Tag, but now that the club is doing business with the Mafia, I've decided to stay in touch by text more than in person.

"I've been super busy," I say, "and so has he."

"Cooking that?" he asks, pointing to my swollen stomach. I rub a hand over my pregnancy bump. "Why have you kept it from us?"

"Because it's none of your business is why," I snap. "You don't even like me, so why the hell do you care if I see Ace or not?"

"Who said I don't like you?" He growls. "I never said that."

"It's in the way you glare at me and the way you always growl in my direction."

"I growl in everyone's direction. I'm a biker, it's what we do." He takes a deep breath, and while I think it's to calm himself, he still looks pissed.

"I'll call him," I mutter, holding up a mug to see if he wants a coffee. He nods a yes, and I set about making it.

"Three sugars," he grumbles. I smile as I add three sugars to each of our cups. At least we have something in common. "I do like you, Lucy," he says, and I get the impression these words are hard for him. He doesn't seem the sentimental type. "I have trust issues, long story, but don't take it personal. I hate seeing Ace like this. He was happy when you showed up, and now you're gone again, he's pissed off with the world and a real dick to be around."

"It shouldn't all be on me," I argue. "He knows where I live, and he can come and see me."

"He's scared your mum might turn up," he says with a smirk.

"My mum doesn't know about him. I didn't tell her because I didn't want to upset her. She's had enough shock with this," I say, prodding my stomach.

"Why don't you bring the father along to meet Ace? We can ask Bernie to cook us a civilised meal." Now, it's my turn to smirk. The Rebellions having a civilised meal doesn't sound right.

"Actually, I'm single. A one-night stand. Tinder has a lot to answer for." Hulk raises his eyebrows in surprise. "Don't judge me. I'm sure you've had your fair share of one-night stands." Hulk laughs and then shrugs his huge shoulders innocently.

"Look, come over, it'll make his day. Besides, this baby will need some family around if you're single, and I know Piper and the girls would love to see you."

I don't mention that I've kept in touch with all three girls. "Fine," I sigh, "let me change."

Half an hour later, I'm walking back into Rebellion clubhouse. The place is empty, but it's Sunday, so I guess the guys are with their families. "Sit here. I can't wait to see his face." Hulk smiles, leading me to the empty bar. I lift myself onto a stool, and he rushes off to find Ace. I tap my fingers impatiently on the bar top. I hear a low moan and glance around the empty room to locate the source of the noise. It happens again, so I get down from the stool and move behind the bar. It seems to be where the noise is coming from, and from the low moans, I'm expecting to find someone injured or sick.

I push the cellar door. It's cold and damp inside. I hope Happy hasn't had an accident, as the beer barrels are so heavy. "Happy," I call out, and the groaning stops. Instead, I hear a muffled giggle. I begin to realise the noise is more likely from pleasure rather than pain, and as I round the stacked barrels, I find the source.

Tag has a female bent over a barrel. He's holding one of her legs up and covering her mouth with his free hand. She's still giggling into his hand, and she doesn't seem too bothered that he's stopped mid-thrust with his eyes fixed on me. We're locked in a stare, me horrified and him shocked.

"Oh my god, I am so sorry," I mutter and then turn and run, my face burning from embarrassment.

I knew Tag was probably fucking his way around London—it's not like he was so heartbroken for me that he'd never have sex again—but to find him like that is painful and not something I ever want to see again.

I crash straight into Ace, who steadies me with his big hands and then smiles wide. "Baby girl, you came back." He grins, wrapping me in a bear hug. He takes a step back, holding me at arm's length and looking me up and down. His eyes fix to my bump. "What the fuck happened?"

I glance behind me, my mind still on Tag. "Erm, one-night stand, complicated," I mumble.

"One-night stand?" repeats Ace.

Hulk grins and laughs. "It's a Tinder baby."

"Oh dear lord," Ace groans. He looks past me, and I know Tag is there. "Have you heard this shit, man? My only daughter is pregnant because of a right swipe."

I feel his presence approach me from behind. "Yeah?" he asks.

"Yeah. Shit, baby girl, is that why you haven't been to see me?"

"I've been busy," I mutter. "I'm sorry. But I did text."

"Without mentioning this bombshell," he points out. My head feels fuzzy and the urge to run away is overwhelming. "Let's not worry about that now. Come and sit. We need a catch up." Ace ushers me towards a couch, and I lower into it. Hulk and Tag sit at the bar, talking in low voices. Ace lifts my feet, placing them on a small coffee table.

"He ain't stupid, baby girl, and neither am I," he says, his face is serious.

"Sorry?" I ask innocently.

"He asked me two months ago how you were, if I'd seen you, and if you were pregnant. He was drunk, but now I realise two things. One, he was the reason you were staying away, and two, he's the baby daddy."

"If you're talking about Tag, you're way off the mark." I laugh, shaking my head.

"You've been avoiding me because you knew he'd be around here. You didn't want him to see you. It surprises me that after what your mother did to me, you being the child who was denied a father, that you'd do the same to Tag."

"That's not fair," I hiss, tears springing to my eyes. "He left me. He was the one who said we wouldn't work and ran out of my room before I even opened my eyes. He's a coward. And if he can run from me, then he'll run from this baby."

"You've denied him a chance to be something better," Ace says calmly. "And you've denied this kid of having a good father."

"Good," I repeat and raise a brow sceptically.

"He was clearly good enough for you at some point because you ended up sleeping with him," snaps Ace. "But yeah, I stand by that, because he is good. He might have to live a different lifestyle, but deep down, he would look after this kid and protect it with everything he has. Your mother judged me the same way, but I can stand before you now and tell you, hand on heart, that I am a good father. I raised Hulk good."

"I know," I mumble, "but he doesn't want me. It was his choice."

"So, because he doesn't want you, he can't see the kid you made together?" I fiddle with my bag, uncomfortable with this conversation. I didn't mean it like that. I'd just decided that if Tag wasn't ready to settle down with me, then he wouldn't want to be a part of this baby. "You'd better come up with a better excuse cos he's coming over," adds Ace, standing.

I grab at his hand. "No, don't leave me," I desperately beg.

He shakes me off, scowling. "You think he's gonna hurt my girl in my own club? You're safe," he reassures me, then he stares at Tag. "Be nice," he warns before leaving me alone with Tag.

TAG

My heart hammers in my chest. I take a seat on the opposite couch because just being this close to Lucy is driving me crazy. For six months, I've pictured her, every morning, every night, and all the hours in-between. "Ten plus one," I eventually say, and she shrugs, avoiding looking at me. "Got anything you want to tell me, Ten?" I want to give her the chance to tell me straight. If she lies, I don't know how I'll react, because we both know the truth.

When Ace mentioned that she hadn't been to see him, I wondered if she was hiding something and I checked up, watched her through her office window. She didn't look pregnant then, but she does now.

"I told you I was gonna join Tinder," she offers feebly.

I slam my hand on the coffee table by her feet, and she jumps in fright. "Don't fucking lie to me, Ten," I growl. Ace steps towards us, but Hulk stops him. "Please, not after everything," I add in a calmer tone.

"I was going to take the morning after pill. It sounds so stupid now, but it was on my to-do list. It just slipped my mind. We got busy in the shop that week, and I was hurt over you leaving, so I was preoccupied." She speaks so quickly that I have trouble processing her words. "I didn't really think much of it. I reasoned that it was just one time, and the chances were so slim." She buries her face in her hands. "I sound like a child," she mumbles.

"Why didn't you tell me?" I ask. I'm not mad that she didn't take the pill—after all, I'm as much to blame—but I'm pissed she didn't tell me.

"I didn't know until about six weeks ago. I was getting my period up until then, but I was putting on weight, so I went for a check-up. The doctor did the test and, well, here we are."

"Lucy, you should have told me. I would have been there for you."

"Out of pity?" she asks. "No, thanks."

"Out of love, not pity. I stepped away because I thought it was the right thing to do, but you being pregnant changes that." It's killed me staying away from her, and I've thrown myself into work and making sure things between the MC and the Mafia stay good.

Lucy stands, snatching up her bag. "No, it changes nothing, Tag. You're still who you are, and I'm still who I am. You didn't ask me what I wanted. You made the choice to walk away, and now, you have to live with that, the same way I do."

"You're telling me that I can't see my own kid?" I snap, also standing.

"I'm saying that I am off the table. You can have contact with the baby if that's what you want."

I sigh. "Of course, that's what I want."

"I'll let you know when it's born," she snaps, heading for the door.

"What? Lucy, wait. We have things to discuss, plans to make."

Callie walks towards me, her lips painted red and her hair fluffed to perfection. She snuggles into my side and smiles up at me. *Talk about bad fucking timing.* Lucy looks at me like she's waiting for me to explain, but I have no words, so she sighs and carries on her mission to leave.

"Who was that chick?" asks Callie.

"My world." I sigh. "My whole fucking world." Callie pouts, and I unwrap her arm from around my waist.

"Well, that was a clusterfuck," says Ace. "I won't come to you for lessons in love."

"Man, she's as stubborn as you are," I huff, and he grins. "You know I'm gonna claim her, right?" His face hardens and he glances to Hulk for backup. Hulk saunters towards me, a smile on his lips.

"Check you out, the gangster using our words. You wanna claim my sister, you have to work for it."

"I have a feeling she'll make me do that without you fuckers getting involved." They both laugh, and I groan. Lucy is gonna be hard work, but now she's got a part of me growing inside her, there's no way I'm leaving her alone.

Chapter Twenty

LUCY

I've squeezed myself into a ridiculous slimline black dress. It's covered in sequins, and I'd instantly loved it, but I didn't consider the lack of stretch in the material now that I'm seven months pregnant.

The room around me is filling up. My mother is flapping around her guests, welcoming them and ensuring everyone has a full glass of Champagne. I hate these functions, but for once, I love the charity that my mother has chosen to help. After many discussions, she settled on a charity that supports families that have suffered from domestic violence. I think hearing my side of things when I finally told her the truth behind me and Noah helped her choice.

Tyra waves to me, as she, Piper, and Bel enter the large hall. We hug in greeting and then settle at our table. "Your mum looks stressed," says Tyra.

"She's always stressed, but she thrives on it."

"I need to tell you something," Piper says, shifting uncomfortably in her seat.

"Does it have anything to do with that hunk of a man who impregnated her?" asks Tyra, staring across the room. I follow her gaze and spot Tag, Scar, Hulk, and Anton making their way through the crowd.

"Oh Piper, what the hell have you done?" I hiss, trying to sink back in my chair.

"It really wasn't me this time, I promise. I spotted his car outside when we arrived."

"I think I might vomit," I groan, watching in horror as the guys take a seat at our table.

"Ladies, you all look amazing," Scar says, grinning.

"What are you doing here?" asks Piper. A shadow falls over her, and Hulk pulls out the seat next to her. She rolls her eyes, shifting her seat farther away from him.

"We paid a lot of money for these seats," says Anton. "It's lovely to see you all."

Tag gets the seat next to me, and I look around for something I can throw up into if the need arises. "You look hot tonight," he whispers close to my ear.

"Tag, what are you doing?" I ask, my voice pained.

"I'm giving money to a great cause."

I sigh. "You know what I mean."

My mother saunters over, glancing around at the handsome men who have joined our table. She kisses my cheek, smiling at Tag. "Darling, you look lovely," she says. "And girls, it's so lovely to see you all."

"I'm Matteo," says Tag, holding out his hand. My mother blushes, and it's nice to see that I'm not the only one affected by his charms. "The father of your soon-to-be grandchild." My smile freezes in an awkward grimace, and the other girls glare at Tag in shock.

"Oh," my mum stammers to find the words she needs. "Darling, shall we talk?" she adds.

I stand, but so does Tag. "I'd like to join."

"No," I snap, "you've done enough." He ignores me and follows my mother. "Oh, dear god, someone help me," I cry, and Piper gives my hand a sympathetic squeeze.

"At least she doesn't know who I am yet." Hulk grins, and I groan louder, following my mother and Tag.

We go into a small office. "Sorry to just spring that on you, but I don't think Lucy was ever going to tell you."

"You are such a snitch," I hiss.

"I appreciate you being honest with me," says my mother sternly. "I don't understand why you're keeping secrets, Lucy. It's good that you have someone."

"I don't," I mutter. "We aren't together."

"I have money, and I'm willing to provide for your daughter and our child," says Tag, and I want to punch him in the face.

My mother smiles. "So, you plan to marry Lucy?"

"Oh my god, Mum," I yell, "please stop."

"I do, yes. Lucy is taking some convincing though," says Tag.

"She's stubborn. She gets it from her father," Mum says, sharing a laugh with Tag.

"I'd like you to join us for dinner soon. I'll arrange it and give the details to Lucy." She continues, "I have to get back to the guests. It was lovely to finally meet you, Matteo." She breezes out of the room, and I'm left staring at Tag open-mouthed.

"What was that?" I snap.

"I'm laying my cards on the table, Ten."

"Stuff your cards. How dare you just turn up and introduce yourself?"

"Ace said she was scary. I thought I should prove how serious I am about us." I growl and then stomp from the room. I really could do with a drink right now.

Piper looks just as annoyed when I return to the table. Hulk is talking into her ear, and she's staring down at her napkin, occasionally shaking her head.

Tag returns, taking the bottle of wine from the centre of the table and filling his glass. He looks annoyed, and I wonder if he expected me to fall into his arms at his declaration of commitment. "You do know that I'll keep turning up, keep harassing you, until I get what I want," he mutters, taking a large gulp of the wine and then wincing at the bitter taste.

"You'll get bored before I do," I say confidently.

"I doubt that, Ten. I'm very persistent when I want something."

"Until you get it, and then . . ." I trail off.

"What does that mean?"

"Well, look at the lengths you went to so you could get Ella. You got her and then you lost interest."

Tag stands suddenly, surprising everyone at the table. He slams his hands on the table. "Fuck you, Lucy. You have no idea." He marches out of the room.

"You know, I could always just have you kidnapped," sighs Anton, his tone bored, "keep you locked at his place."

"The best thing you can do is tell him to give up," I hiss.

Anton stares me down, and even though I'm annoyed and hormonal, I quake at the warning in his eyes. "You don't want to cross me, Lucy."

"You don't want to threaten my sister," growls Hulk, and Piper practically swoons next to him.

The dinner is brought to the table and the waitress begins to serve. We sit in silence. Tag returns, drinks more wine, and pushes his food away. I wish for the hundredth time that I'd stayed at home in my pyjamas.

TAG

Why is it so hard? I used to click my fingers and have women drop at my feet. The one woman I want, and she's determined to keep me away. "What was that between you and Piper?" I ask, glancing in the rear-view mirror at Hulk as we drive home.

"She's met a guy. I found out."

"What's wrong with that?" asks Anton.

"Nothing, I just wanted to remind her that if she goes on the date, she and I can never happen again."

"You and Piper are a thing?" asks Anton in surprise.

"No, we hook up sometimes. She's free to go with any man she wants, but she won't be climbing back into my bed."

"Sounds to me like you like her a whole lot more than you're letting on," I say.

"Like you know anything about women. How did it go tonight?" asks Hulk sarcastically.

"It just takes time. She'll come round eventually."

Anton slows the vehicle to a stop outside my apartment block. "You want us to come up?" he asks.

"No, man, I'm good. Thanks for coming tonight."

I step outside to light a cigarette. I hear the roar of a motorbike heading my way, and as I glance to the left, I see the headlight slowing down. I half-turn to see what the hell is going on. Anton must think it's suspicious too because his car slows down.

I don't react quick enough when I see the gun. I know it's pointing at me, but I freeze, my legs suddenly feeling like stone. The sound of the shot ricochets off the surrounding buildings, and a second shot rings out as the first rips into my stomach.

I always go out in a bulletproof vest, but tonight, I left it home because it made my suit look too bulky. I smile to myself at the thought, such a strange thing to think about in all this chaos.

I fall to the ground and everything moves in slow motion. The second bullet hits my leg, but the pain from my stomach is much worse, and I grip the wound with both hands. Looking down at the blood pouring between my fingers, I try to feel for the hole so I can plug it better. The sound of rubber screeching, followed by another shot, has me craning my neck to see what's going on. The biker is already away, and Anton's bullet misses him.

Scar drops down by my side. He's yelling into his phone for a doctor while ripping his shirt over his head. He drops his mobile to press his shirt to my wound, and I smile at him gratefully. I try to talk, but nothing comes out. Instead, I lay my head against the cool ground. It suddenly feels too heavy, and my eyes are tired. "Tag, don't close your eyes, brother. Stay with me."

I'd love to stay, but it's such hard work. I try to open my eyes again, I really do. I hear Anton shouting my name and I try to lift my hand so I can reassure him that I'm not scared, but that too feels like lead.

The voices grow distant until I don't hear anything . . . just silence. It's nice to finally feel at peace. It's been far too long since I've felt this relaxed and free, and as I give in to the pull of eternal peace, I see Lucy.

She looks sad, and she's holding out her hand to me. Tears stain her pale face as her other hand cradles her neat bump. Her mouth is moving, but I can't hear her words. I feel like I'm floating as I move towards her, and as I get closer, I see her mouth the word *'stay'*.

Chapter Twenty-One

♥

LUCY

My mobile rings and I moan, reaching for the bedside table with my eyes still firmly closed tight. I feel around until it's in my hand and then blindly put it to my ear. "Hello," I croak.

"Baby girl, it's Ace. I'm at your door, please open up."

"What time is it?"

"It's three in the morning. I wouldn't be here if it wasn't important."

Adrenaline pumps through my body and I rush to open the door. Ace steps inside, looking out of place in my small apartment. "It's Tag."

"Is he okay?" When he doesn't answer, panic sets in. "Dad. is he okay?" It's the first time I've used this title for him, and it feels right, even if the timing is wrong.

"It's not looking good, Lucy. We should go to the hospital. He was shot."

I hate hospitals. The smell, the dull paint on the walls, the constant beeping of machines keeping people alive. I rub my arms and pace back and forth. The waiting room is busy. Saturday nights in London can get messy, people can't handle their alcohol these days.

When I arrived, Tag had already gone into surgery. All I can think about is the last time I saw him and how I would do anything to have this night all over again so I can forgive him. *I thought I'd have more time to forgive him.* I place my hand on my stomach and feel the baby wriggle around.

When the doctor approaches, we all stand. "Mr. Martinez," he says to Anton, "follow me and I'll update you."

I go to follow, but Anton shakes his head. "Stay here."

"No, I want to know what's going on," I snap, and he raises a warning eyebrow in my direction. "Anton, please." I'm not ashamed to beg, I'm so desperate for news.

Anton nods to Ace, who takes me by the arm. "Stay here. Anton will update us." I sigh, knowing I'll never get my own way if they're all in agreement, so I take a seat and watch Anton and the doctor disappear into a side room.

He's gone for around five minutes, but it feels like hours before he reappears. We all look in his direction expectantly. He locks eyes with Ace, and then shakes his head once. I glance back and forth between the two. "What?" I ask. "What does that mean?" I can feel myself getting hysterical. "What the fuck does that mean?"

"Lucy," says Ace, his face twisted in agony, "I'm so sorry."

"For what? I don't understand." Ace takes my hands and gently rubs the back of them with his thumbs. "Please," I whisper. "Please, Dad, he's not gone." I'm sobbing as he wraps me in his large embrace.

"Let's get you out of here. You need privacy," he whispers into my hair.

"I want to see him," I cry. "I need to see him." Anton shakes his head again, and Ace sighs. "Don't you tell me no! You are *not* the boss of me," I scream towards Anton. I'm sick of him calling the shots. "Where were you? Why didn't you protect him?"

Ace begins to lead me away. "Baby girl, now is not the time."

Ace takes me back to the clubhouse. I'm wrapped in a blanket and placed on the couch with Piper and Queenie either side of me, whispering words of comfort.

I replay our last time together at the charity function and begin to cry again. Queenie goes to make tea, telling me sweet tea is exactly what I need. But that's not true. I need him . . . I need Tag.

"You have a room here, Lucy," says Ace. "Anton doesn't want you left alone until he knows who is behind the attack on Tag."

"Murder," I mutter. "It was murder." He hangs his head and then gives a nod. "We need to speak to the police."

"No. Anton is dealing with it, Lucy, the police aren't involved."

"Not involved? Are you serious?" I screech. "He was shot down in the street, how can the police not know about it?"

"They know—it's just how things are done. You know he wasn't legit, so we do this Anton's way."

"Fuck Anton! Get me my phone," I yell.

Piper takes my hand. "Listen," she begins, "I know this is awful, and I have no idea how you feel right now, but let's trust Anton on this. He knows what he's doing. If you still feel the same tomorrow, then we'll call Anton and discuss it with him. He isn't going to let the people who did this get away with it. Tag was his best friend." I know she's right. Anton and Tag were close.

Queenie brings me my tea, and I take a sip. My heart hurts so bad and I just want to be alone.

The days blur into one. I spend time with Ace, and it's the only good thing to come out of this whole sorry situation. I don't hear or see anything of Anton, which frustrates me. I'd at least like an update on the funeral. Even though Tag and I weren't a thing, I'm still carrying his child and I'd still like to say my goodbyes. He'd want me to be there, I know he would.

I close my eyes as Piper runs a brush through my freshly washed hair. She and Queenie have taken it upon themselves to make sure I get up and dressed every day, as well as eat something. They're doing it because they care, but a part of me wishes I was at home in my apartment so I could hide away from the world. In a few days' time, I'll be eight months pregnant, just a month away from giving birth. The thought brings fresh tears to my eyes. "We should think about going shopping for the baby. Have you got anything yet?" asks Piper.

I shake my head. I hadn't known for very long and then all this happened with Tag. I don't think I have it in me to go shopping and look at baby things. This should be a happy time.

Ace wanders over, looking sheepish. "Tyra and Bel are here to see you, darling," he says. "Anton is with them."

I push myself to sit up straighter, looking over to the bar area where I see the three of them. "Does Anton have news?"

"Sort of," says Ace. "Let's go into my office."

TAG

I open my eyes. The light is blinding, and I instantly squeeze them shut again. "Tag." It's Anton's voice. "Are you awake?" I open them again, but this time, I blink until they adjust to the lighting. I'm in a bedroom, but it's not my own. "You're at my place," explains Anton. He looks tired and stressed, and his hair is messy, like he's been running his fingers through it. "Man, did you give me a scare." He sighs, taking a seat at the side of my bed.

"Ten," I croak. I need to see Lucy.

"Long story, Tag. I'll fill you in once the doc's been in to check you over. Doc," he yells. The Rebellion's club doctor enters, gives me a smile, and then presses some buttons on a machine at the side of the bed. It beeps and then something on my arm squeezes tight.

"Just checking your blood pressure," he explains.

"What happened?" I whisper, my throat so dry that it's hard to get the words out.

"You were shot," Doc explains. "It's been a tough week."

I think back to the charity function. Ten was annoyed with me, and I drank too much wine. We left on bad terms, and I was frustrated with her. I remember getting out of Anton's car and walking towards my apartment block, and I remember the motorbike. I turn to Anton. "Did you get him yet?"

Anton shakes his head. "No, man. We're close, though."

"You're doing well, Tag. A few more days rest and I think you'll be up and about. You'll need to take it slow, no jumping into the fighting ring for a while, but considering what happened, you're very lucky."

"I want to see Lucy," I repeat.

The doc and Anton exchange a wary look, and then the doc leaves. "About that," mutters Anton. "She thinks you're dead." The beeping noise on the machine gets faster and I try to sit up. Anton places a hand on my chest, pushing me to lie down again. "Hear me out, Tag." He waits for me to settle down. "We don't know who put the hit out on you. I put the word out that it was successful because I'm trying to keep you alive. Until I know who wants you dead, it's better for them to think they're winning."

"She must be out of her mind," I growl. "You could have told her."

"You know I can't, and you'd do exactly the same if you were in my shoes. I wasn't sure if whoever did this was around at the hospital or had inside men. I needed it to look real, and Lucy couldn't have fake cried. She had to think you were dead."

"She's pregnant. What if the stress harms the baby?" I snap.

"Doc is keeping an eye on her. She's staying with Ace so he can look after her. Queenie and Piper are making sure she's okay."

"Do they know?"

"Ace and Doc are the only people who know."

"You have to tell her, Ant. You can't do this to her, and I can't be a ghost forever. She's having my kid, I want to be a part of that."

"I know, and we'll tell her. I didn't want to give her false hope. You were pretty close to knocking on the devil's door man."

"Well, now I'm awake, you can bring her to me."

"I can't have her leave the club. She might be in danger too, especially if the news is out there that she's pregnant with your kid. Once you're on your feet, you can go and see her."

"No, Anton, this won't wait. Go and tell her the truth."

LUCY

I take a seat on the worn couch in Ace's office. Tyra and Bel each hold my hand as Anton paces before us. "Anton, please just tell us.

You're worrying us," says Bel. He looks directly at her, and for the first time, I see something else in his eyes, maybe a fondness.

"I'm just gonna come right out and say this," he begins. "I lied."

"About?" asks Tyra.

"About Tag. He's not dead." The room begins to spin, and I grip the girls' hands tighter. "I had to lie to keep him safe."

"What the fuck are you talking about?" growls Tyra.

"I needed everyone to think Tag was dead because I don't know who wants him dead."

I feel nauseous and my stomach tightens. "What?" I croak.

"I'm sorry, Lucy. I needed it to look real, and you had to look devastated at the hospital in case anyone was watching."

"Tag's not dead?" I repeat. Anton shakes his head. He stops pacing and places his hands on his hips. His head hangs like he's ashamed, but I know he's not. He's too up himself to feel shame.

I dive from the chair, causing it to crash to the floor, and as my hand rakes across his cheek, I feel a mild satisfaction. "You bastard," I scream.

Anton hisses, but I don't wait for him to react. Instead, I punch him hard on the nose. It doesn't bleed like I'd hoped it would, but it makes him growl, and that's good enough for me. Arms wrap around me and I'm gently pulled back against Hulk's body. It's the first time I've seen him since the night of the attack as he went on a run after leaving the hospital.

He grins. "Now, now, let's not damage his ugly face too much."

"How dare you put me through that?" I scream, "You make me sick!"

"I had to, Lucy. You don't understand," he explains, keeping a hand over the now bleeding scratches on his cheek.

"I understand perfectly. It would have suited you, wouldn't it? You wanted me out of the way."

Anton sighs. "That's not true."

"Where is he? Take me to him now."

"I can't do that, not yet."

"To hell you can't. You take me to him now, or I'll call the police and tell them how you've covered up his attack."

Anton laughs and shakes his head. "Tag was right to try and walk away from you. You don't understand our life, and you'd never cope with it." He leaves the office, and I turn in Hulk's arms, sobbing and burying my face into his chest, taking him by surprise.

When Ace comes in, he still looks sheepish. "I know this is fucked up," he begins, and I realise he knew about it, "but Anton was protecting his family."

"Tag is not his family. This is his family," I snap, pointing to my stomach. "How could you watch me break like that and not tell me?"

"I couldn't, Lucy. I wanted to, trust me. I was trying to do the right thing."

"By lying to me? I thought we were getting on well," I snap.

"We are."

"No, you ruined it with your lies. Your priority should be me, not that piece of shit just because he's in some stupid Mafia!"

"Now, you listen to me," growls Ace, squaring his shoulders and pasting a stern look on his face. "I went along with it to protect you all. I know Tag means a lot to you, and because of that, I agreed to help keep him alive. Anton didn't know who was trying to kill him and didn't want someone trying to come and finish the job. I know you don't get our world or the way we do shit, but it's just the way it is. If you love Tag, then you'd better get used to it." He stomps out of the room grumbling to himself.

Chapter Twenty-Two

TAG

I smirk as Anton rubs a hand over his scratches. It's been two days since I woke up and this is the first day I've been able to get out of bed without wanting to vomit. Today, I'm being transferred to the Rebellion clubhouse.

Anton is convinced that my father is behind the hit, which is a real kick in the nuts after everything I did to keep him alive. Now, with Conner out of the way, Anton thinks he wants to come back and take his place. We have men hunting him down, but the threat is still high, so I'm going to the Rebellions to stay until I've made a good recovery. Lucy hasn't picked up any calls from me. She's taken the news hard, and Ace thinks she needs time. Well, unfortunately for her, the time is up. Too much has happened, and I'll be damned if I waste any more time. Lucy is mine, and from today, she'll know it.

I'm taken down to the private, underground car park under Anton's home. I leave in a car with blacked-out windows and under the armed care of some of our men. Anton is leaving nothing to chance. Arriving at the back of the clubhouse, I'm taken inside in a wheelchair because I'm too slow on crutches.

Ace greets me with a handshake and a pat on the shoulder. "Good to see you alive, brother." He smiles. "Maybe you can cheer up my girl now because she's ignoring me and pretty much refusing to leave her room."

"Point me in that direction," I say, "but please don't let it be on the top floor."

Luckily, Lucy's room is on the first floor, and I just about manage the stairs. I tap lightly on her door, but she doesn't answer. I go on in and find her laying with her back to the door. "Are you gonna lay in here being mad for much longer?" I ask casually. She spins to face me, a look of pure shock on her face. "Mind if I climb in there with yah? Those stairs killed me," I joke, using my crutches to make my way to the bed.

Lucy stands, throwing her arms around me and almost causing me to lose my balance. "Oh god, you don't know how good it is to see you," she sobs, burying her face into my neck. "I never thought I'd see you again."

"You have no faith." I grin. "Even death can't keep me from you."

"It's too soon for jokes," she mumbles into my neck. "I'm still very mad about that."

I hold her against me and lower to sit on her bed, pulling her with me. She snuggles against my chest. "Baby, for us to work, you have to understand, shit's done differently. Anton did the right thing at the time. Granted, he should have told you sooner, but he was busy trying to find the culprit."

"I don't care, what he did was cruel."

"He did what was necessary to keep me alive. He's a good man, and he's also part of my life. The organisation is a part of my life, and you have to accept that for us to work."

"I don't like lies, Tag."

"Nobody does. I won't lie to you, I promise, but sometimes, you might not get the full truth. I can't promise that I can tell you everything. In fact, there will be times when I'll be here but my mind will be elsewhere and I won't be able to tell you any of it. You'll see things in me that you'll hate, like when I came to you covered in blood. I can't tell you any of that because it implicates you. But please believe that everything I do will be to keep you safe . . . you and this little one."

Lucy places a gentle kiss on my cheek. "I don't have a choice. I can't be away from you, not now that I know what it feels like to be without you. I prayed to have you back, and now, I've got you. We'll work through it."

"And Anton?" I ask.

"I can't promise to roll over and obey him, we don't like each other, but I'll try."

I pull her in for a deeper kiss, breathing in her vanilla scent. I never thought I'd feel her in my arms again. When I laid on the ground with my blood spilling out, I thought it was the end. I have another chance, and I'm gonna make us work.

LUCY

I lay staring at Tag as he sleeps. He looks peaceful, but I can still see the paleness in his skin tone and the dark circles under his eyes. He looked frail when he first walked into my room this evening. It broke my heart all over again.

"Stop staring at me," he croaks sleepily.

"No," I say with a smile, "I'm never taking my eyes off you again."

"You joke, but that's what'll happen from now on. I'll be watching your every move."

"Stalker." I smile, kissing him on the head.

We have yet to leave my room. We spent hours making love, getting to know each other all over again. I reach for Tag's painkillers from the bedside table and pop a few into my hand. "Take your meds," I say, reaching for the glass of water.

Tag swallows the tablets and then places a kiss on my bump. The baby kicks, and he smiles up at me. "You feel that?" He grins, placing another kiss.

"It's an active little thing." I smile, rubbing my hand over the bump. I can finally look forward to our baby and vow to go and buy everything we need as soon as Tag is feeling up to getting out. The thought of hit men popping up when we're shopping wipes the smile from my face. "Will we have to spend the rest of our lives looking over our shoulders, Tag?"

"I hope not, baby. Now that Conner is dead, things will be different. Anton wants to take the organisation on a different path. I'm not saying we're suddenly gonna become advocates for the police force or anything, but maybe we'll be able to sleep better at night."

"You two lovebirds finished in there?" A bang on the door accompanies the shout that sounds like Hulk. "We're having a few drinks in the bar, come down."

"Is that an order?" asks Tag.

"Damn straight," Hulk replies.

I help Tag down the stairs and pass him his crutches at the bottom. As we enter the bar, everyone cheers, raising glasses in our direction. "Good to see you smile, Luce," says Ace, kissing me on the cheek.

"I'm sorry for being such a bitch," I whisper as he hugs me. "I get it."

"It killed me lying to you like that, and I promise I won't do it again." He shakes hands with Tag. "Take care of my baby girl. I've only just got her back."

Tag grins at me. "I plan to, Ace, don't you worry about that."

Epilogue

LUCY

Three weeks later, I cradle my baby son in my arms and smile over at Tag. He's looking so much better. His limp is almost gone, and the only real sign that he was shot is the two small scars, one on his stomach and the other on his thigh.

He began training a couple weeks ago, just gentle exercises to get him back in shape. I know he's frustrated, wanting his recovery to be much quicker, but I've enjoyed having him with me all the time instead of at the gym.

We're still staying at the Rebellion clubhouse, and honestly, I love it here. I'm in no rush to go back to my apartment. Being here means there's always someone around to help with Abel, and there's always someone to talk to. Piper's become a really good friend and seeing her every day is amazing.

My mother wasn't too happy when I first told her where I was living these days, but she's learning to accept it. When I mentioned that Ace was still single, her eyes sparkled, but she's yet to see him face to face.

"I can't wait to drink Prosecco again." I sigh dreamily. Breastfeeding means that Tag is against me having a drop of alcohol in case I pass it on to his pride and joy and Abel ends up drunk. He's so overprotective, but I wouldn't change it for the world.

Mae doesn't respond. I follow her dreamy stare to where Ace is chatting with Hulk. "Please don't tell me you're crushing on Hulk too," I groan. It's bad enough that he and Piper dance in circles, pretending to hate each other.

"What?" she asks, snapping from her daydream. "Oh god, no, I wasn't staring at him."

I laugh. "Well, I know you weren't staring at Ace. He's old enough to be your dad."

She laughs too, shaking her head. "Of course not."

She avoids my quizzical stare, fiddling with Abel's little toes as he sleeps soundly in my arms. I don't have a chance to investigate further because Tag leans down, taking Abel from me and handing him to Mae. "Stand," he orders, and I don't question him because he's always bossing me around. I stare in disbelief when Tag drops down on to one knee.

"What are you doing, Tag?" I hiss.

"I've had to wait so long to do this, but now my leg is finally feeling stronger, I can get down on one knee." I glance around. the whole room is quiet and everyone is staring at us. "Ten, will you marry me?"

Tears form in my eyes as he takes my hand and slips a diamond ring on my finger. "I haven't said yes yet." I smile.

"Oh, I only asked to be polite, Ten. I already have my answer."

I laugh as he stands and pulls me against his hard chest. "Well, the answer is yes, just in case you were confused." I grin.

Clapping and cheers erupt around us as Tag picks me up and swings me around. "I love you, Ten." He smiles, kissing me hard on the lips.

"I love you too, Matteo, but we really need to think about revising my low score."

"You're a ten out of ten, baby."

THE END

A note from me to you

♥

Tag was originally released back in 2019 under the title Rebellion MC. When I received it back from my old publisher this year, I wasn't sure whether to release it again, but there are a few readers that still message me about this series now, wanting me to add to it. So, after a new cover and some new edits, I'm putting him back out there into the world. I hope you enjoy him.

I'm a UK author, based in Nottinghamshire. I live with my husband of many years, our two teenage boys and our four little dogs. I write MC and Mafia romance with plenty of drama and chaos. I also love to read similar books. Before I became a full-time author, I was a teaching assistant working in a primary school.

If you'd like to follow my writing journey, join my readers group on Facebook, the link is above. You can also use that link if you're a book blogger, I'd love you to sign up to my team.

Popular Books by Nicola Jane

The Kings Reapers MC

Riggs' Ruin https://mybook.to/RiggsRuin
Capturing Cree https://mybook.to/CapturingCree
Wrapped in Chains https://mybook.to/WrappedinChains
Saving Blu https://mybook.to/SavingBlu
Riggs' Saviour https://mybook.to/RiggsSaviour
Taming Blade https://mybook.to/TamingBlade
Misleading Lake https://mybook.to/MisleadingLake
Surviving Storm https://mybook.to/SurvivingStorm
Ravens Place https://mybook.to/RavensPlace
Playing Vinn https://mybook.to/PlayingVinn

The Perished Riders MC

Maverick https://mybook.to/Maverick-Perished

Scar https://mybook.to/Scar-Perished
Grim https://mybook.to/Grim-Perished
Ghost https://mybook.to/GhostBk4
Dice https://mybook.to/DiceBk5
Arthur https://mybook.to/ArthurNJ

<u>The Hammers MC (Splintered Hearts Series)</u>

Cooper https://mybook.to/CooperSHS
Kain https://mybook.to/Kain
Tanner https://mybook.to/TannerSH

Printed in Dunstable, United Kingdom